After the Sunset

FICTION

MEDIA TIE-INS

After the Sunset

A NOVEL BY
Kevin Ryan
A Brett Ratner Film
Story by Paul Zbyszewski
Screenplay by Paul Zbyszewski
and Craig Rosenberg

BERKLEY BOULEVARD BOOKS, NEW YORK

THE BERKLEY PUBLISHING GROUP
Published by the Penguin Group, Penguin Group (USA) Inc., 375 Hudson Street, New York, New York 10014, USA.

Penguin Group (Canada), 10 Alcorn Avenue, Toronto, Ontario, Canada M4V 3B2 (a division of Pearson Penguin Canada Inc.); Penguin Books Ltd., 80 Strand, London WC2R 0RL, England; Penguin Group Ireland, 25 St. Stephen's Green, Dublin 2, Ireland (a division of Penguin Books, Ltd.); Penguin Group (Australia), 250 Camberwell Road, Camberwell, Victoria 3124, Australia (a division of Pearson Australia Group Pty., Ltd.); Penguin Books India Pvt. Ltd., 11 Community Centre, Panchsheel Park, New Delhi—110 017, India; Penguin Group (NZ), Cnr. Airborne and Rosedale Roads, Albany, Auckland, New Zealand (a division of Pearson New Zealand, Ltd.); Penguin Books (South Africa) (Pty.) Ltd., 24 Sturdee Avenue, Rosebank, Johannesburg 2196, South Africa

Penguin Books Ltd., Registered Offices: 80 Strand, London, WC2R 0RL, England

This is a work of fiction. Names, characters, places, and incidents either are the product of the author's imagination or are used fictitiously, and any resemblance to actual persons, living or dead, business establishments, events, or locales is entirely coincidental.

AFTER THE SUNSET

A Berkley Boulevard Book / published by arrangement with New Line Productions, Inc.

PRINTING HISTORY
Berkley Boulevard movie tie-in-edition / October 2004

Copyright © 2004 by New Line Productions, Inc.
Interior text design by Tiffany Estreicher

ISBN: 0-425-20141-4

BERKLEY® BOULEVARD
Berkley Boulevard Books are published by The Berkley Publishing Group,
a division of Penguin Group (USA) Inc.,
375 Hudson Street, New York, New York 10014.
BERKLEY BOULEVARD is a trademark belonging to Penguin Group (USA) Inc.

PRINTED IN THE UNITED STATES OF AMERICA

10 9 8 7 6 5 4 3 2 1

Chapter One

A black carry case sat open on the table. The case was very strong. It was made of titanium but covered on the outside in finely crafted leather while the inside was custom formed for its contents and lined with silk. The box was impressive enough in its own way, but it was nothing compared to what it contained: a large diamond, apparently flawless, and glittering brightly even in the dull fluorescent lighting of the office.

One of the security men carefully and gently closed the case, instinctively treating it with great care. When the lid was closed, he inserted a key card. A small click sounded and the box was secure.

* * *

For the hundredth time, Agent Carlson scanned the area with his binoculars as his partner sitting beside him in the stands did the same. Los Angeles' Staples Center arena sat more than twelve thousand. Today, it was full to capacity, but many of the fans were spending little time in their seats. The Lakers and the Clippers were waging a hard-fought battle. It was a very physical game, lots of elbowing and bumping, even a few scuffles.

The crowd was loud, raucous. They were doing their best to shout the Lakers to a victory—though the outcome was never really in doubt. Not surprisingly, the Lakers were dominating. Technically the Staples Center was home for both teams, but the vast majority of the fans were cheering the Lakers.

Still, the game was exciting. Like almost all West Coast teams, the Lakers and Clippers played offensive, running games. That meant high scores and higher spirits for the fans and the players. Even among the screaming fans, one stood out. He was a man in his indeterminate thirties or forties, with a big walrus-style mustache and a large cowboy hat. He was by far the loudest person in his section, and the looks he got from the other fans made it clear that he was obnoxious even by their loose standards.

"Let's go, boys. Put some points up, smoke these guys," the fan shouted.

Carlson ignored the man and looked deeper into the crowd. He quickly found his target. Max Burdett was sitting in his seat, wearing a Lakers cap and holding a hot dog. Burdett was somewhere in his forties, very fit with just the beginnings of grey in his dark hair. The file said he was Irish, but to Carlson he looked like British aristocracy with his *GQ* good looks. At the moment he looked completely relaxed, as if he was enjoying the game quietly.

Of course, Carlson knew that wasn't true. He had only been doing his job a short time, but his instincts told him that Burdett wasn't here for the game. Thanks to the efforts of one Agent Stanley P. Lloyd, there was a large file back at the Bureau that supported that notion. For obvious reasons, the FBI had watched Burdett's movements closely for years. There were records of his habits, his likes, his dislikes, and even a detailed psych file that talked in depth about his moods.

But for Carlson, the most important piece of information was the one that the file did not contain: as far as the Bureau knew—and on this subject the Bureau knew just about everything—Max Burdett was not a basketball fan.

Burdett wasn't going anywhere, at least not while Carlson was watching. Lifting his sleeve, Carlson spoke clearly into the microphone. "Target is in sight," he said.

Special Agent Stanley P. Lloyd got the report from the passenger seat of the Bureau SUV security transport and replied immediately into the radio, "Clock him close."

"He's not going anywhere," Carlson said, his voice in that grey area between confidence and bravado. Stan recognized the tone. There was a time when he had even used it on a case involving Max Burdett. Stan wouldn't make that mistake again. These days, he was more cautious than confident, more careful than he thought he would ever be when he was planning his career in the Bureau—a career that he was sure would be punctuated by big cases, daring arrests, and heavy risk heavily rewarded by his superiors. For a while, his career had been just that.

And then he had met Max Burdett.

A lot had changed since then; Stan had changed since then. Of all the setbacks he had suffered because of their first meeting, Stan resented the changes in himself the most. He had lost a lot of that bravado, the confidence. Some nights he told himself that his new caution made him a more mature and ultimately a more effective agent.

That thought was always followed by a little voice that told him he was full of shit.

Stan knew he had lost his edge. And he also knew that that wasn't likely to change until he had Burdett under arrest and in jail. Many times he had allowed himself to imagine his gloating visits to Burdett in prison. Those thoughts were unprofessional, unworthy of a special agent of the FBI, but they felt pretty damn good and never failed to cheer him up.

Well, if this operation went as well as he expected, he would be pretty damned cheery. In fact, the Bureau might have to have the smile surgically removed from his face. He glanced at his partner Mitch in the driver's seat. Then he turned to the two private security guards sitting in the backseat, the small black carry case that contained the diamond sitting on the seat between them. Sometimes, agents had trouble working with private security, but not Stan, at least not this time. The owners of the diamond had insisted, and as far as Stan was concerned, the more the merrier: the more people he had on his side, the better his chances of success.

Plus, Burdett had an uncanny knowledge of Bureau protocol and tactics. The rent-a-cops would be another x-factor for Burdett. And, each man was highly trained with either military or SWAT background and each carried a semiautomatic MP5—a Heckler & Koch submachine gun favored by local law enforcement. It had a thirty-round capacity and used ten-millimeter cartridges.

It was a helluva weapon. And would give Burdett a helluvan x-factor—thirty ten-millimeter x-factors each, to be exact. However, Stan doubted that they would be necessary. Guns weren't in Burdett's MO and were not Stan's preferred method of closing this case. His dreams for Burdett were not of a quick, final finish, but of a long, lingering prison sentence. Of course, when push came to shove, Stan knew that he would take what he could get.

Stan realized that he was sweating as he watched the odometer tick off tenths of a mile. From the driver's seat, Mitch glanced at him and said, "Relax. We're nearly there." Mitch's voice rang with confidence, but he could afford it—he was young. Stan kept his senses sharp.

Lloyd reached for the console in front of him and switched on the system. A small green light came on and a soothing female voice said, "Good afternoon. Your FBI Travel Link system is now activated. I can assist you with all aspects of your travel. Please choose from the following options."

A list of options appeared on the LCD screen: MUSIC, HEAT, AIR CONDITIONER, LOCKS, EMERGENCY HELP, WINDOWS, BRAKES, IGNITION, and a few others.

Stan knew the system was state-of-the-art, computerizing every aspect of the car's function and providing GPS locators and maps of any street in the country instantly. Stan remembered that much from the briefing, but he had never bothered to read the manual or take the online tutorial. Like all agents, he depended on computers to track down leads and narrow suspect lists. The federal crime database called the National Crime Information Center, or NCIC, had literally changed the job for him in his twenty years with the Bureau. He prided himself on staying current on the software and learning new systems, something older agents often had trouble doing. He was smart enough to get help wherever he could, but he did not need a computer to help him drive a car—at least not yet.

Fortunately, all he needed at the moment was to turn the air-conditioning up. He hit the right button on the screen and waited. Nothing happened. He hit it again. Still nothing. Stan had to restrain himself from punching the damn thing.

"I don't understand your command," the pleasant female voice said.

"Thing's too damned complicated," he snapped.

The Staples Center was now less than two blocks

ahead of them. Stan turned around to make sure the other vehicles were in place. They were; behind him were three more identical security SUVs. Four cars, eight officers, and eight more heavily armed private security men— plenty more x-factors for Mr. Burdett.

The car stopped at a light and immediately a homeless man with a squeegee approached them. Mitch tried to wave him off, but the man slopped the window with the soapy water, running the squeegee over the glass. Stan shook his head. The man was heavily bearded, dressed in rags, and—most importantly—in their way.

Finished cleaning the window, the homeless man held out a gnarled hand. Mitch ignored him, and the man knocked on the window in protest.

"Tip him. Get him outta here," Stan said.

"I only have twenties," Mitch said. It was bullshit, of course, but Stan didn't have time to argue—and he didn't want to spend another second held up by a bum with a squeegee.

The light turned green and Stan cursed under his breath as he dug into his right pants pocket. He pulled out a crumpled dollar bill and passed it to the driver. "You're a cheap bastard, Mitch. Short arms, deep pockets."

The homeless guy smiled in thanks, revealing hideous yellow teeth. In gratitude, the bum gave the windshield another sweep with the squeegee.

"Let's roll," Stan said. He realized he was sweating even harder than before. He was jumpy, too jumpy. He willed himself to stay sharp. He couldn't let a squeegee guy get to him.

He had much bigger fish to fry.

After he made the last pass on the windshield, the homeless man flipped the switch on the handle of the squeegee. Agent Lloyd looked right at him one last time. Of course there was no recognition there. All Lloyd saw was a bum in rags, one who was holding him up and at the moment nothing but a big irritation.

Special Agent Lloyd didn't know the half of it. The smile the homeless man shot him was genuine, but he only looked away in disgust.

Checking the small LCD screen in the handle, the homeless man confirmed that the bar code reader had acquired the SUV's VIN, or vehicle identification number. Without the number, the job would stop right here— there was no second chance to get the VIN.

There was a confirmation beep and the homeless man relaxed, hitting the button to transmit. The screen read TRANSMITTING, VIN BCL9434.

That was it. There were still a hundred things that could go wrong from here, but what happened next was out of the homeless man's hands. The riskiest part of the job was still to come, and it was all up to Max now.

The basketball game was heating up, and Agent Carlson had to work to ignore the action on the court, concentrating instead on Burdett, who was still sitting there looking relaxed. Leaning forward, Carlson took a quick look at the court to catch up on the action. There was a loose ball with both teams racing toward it. The ball shot out-of-bounds mid-court and the ref called it the Clippers' ball. Carlson could see right away that it was a bad call. A fan nearby apparently felt the same way.

"Are you kidding me? That's Lakers' ball! Lakers' ball!" he screamed over at the ref, who simply ignored him. The fan continued, "Don't worry about it, Lakes. One bad call ain't gonna hurt a champion! Shake it off, fellas, come on now."

Finally, the fan sat back down. Carlson saw him take a sip of his drink.

The play began again on the court. The Lakers' point guard Gary Payton set up just outside the point. He moved up and got a pass, turned and drove strong toward the basket. The ref blew his whistle and called a charge on Payton. It was Clippers' ball now.

The angry fan from earlier leapt out of his seat, spilling his drink on the fans in front of him and knocking popcorn out of the hands of someone next to him. Carlson knew this was headed to a bad place.

"Charge? Charge!" the fan shouted. "I'll show you a charge!"

Carlson forced himself to relax. There was no reason for him to get involved. Arena security could handle an angry drunk without him. The fan pushed his way to the aisle, pissing off pretty much everyone in his way, ranting and raving as he went. When he got to the aisle, he started shouting at the court and a few seconds later Staples security arrived.

Carlson did not have to hear them to know that the two security officers were politely asking the fan to return to his seat, but he wouldn't budge. Then the two men started to physically help him back to his seat.

"Let go of me! I paid good money for these seats! Get your hands off me!"

By now the players on the court had noticed the disturbance, and uniformed police officers were racing down to get the man. The angry fan still refused to budge, even when the uniforms arrived.

Suddenly, Carlson realized that he hadn't looked over at Burdett in much too long and quickly scanned the crowd for his target. Burdett was watching the disturbance with his typical cool detachment. *Lloyd was right. He's a smug son of a bitch,* Carlson thought.

Glancing back at the angry fan, Carlson saw that the fan was now in handcuffs and being led up the aisle. For him, the game was over and this was just the beginning of a very long day.

Carlson tracked his binoculars back to Burdett's section. It took him a second to find Burdett . . .

No, more than a second. Carlson found Burdett's seat. It was empty. He quickly scanned the row and the aisle nearby. It was impossible. Burdett couldn't have disappeared in the few seconds Carlson had been looking away.

But impossible or not, Burdett was gone.

"Shit!" he said to his partner who was sitting next to him, as Carlson continued to scan the area for Burdett. "Have you got him?" Carlson asked.

"No, lost him for a sec," his partner replied.

Carlson had a sick feeling in his stomach, but he couldn't wait another second. He lifted his sleeve and spoke into the radio's microphone, "We've lost him. He's gone!"

Agent Lloyd had briefed them all, and Carlson had read all of the reports, but he had been completely confident, certain that the smug bastard would never get by him.

Carlson cursed again and searched furiously with his binoculars and then his naked eyes—knowing, even as he did it, that it was hopeless. Burdett had beaten him. Carlson only hoped that this was Burdett's last victory of the day.

"What?" Stan shouted into the radio. He wanted to pound the dash of the SUV.

"Burdett is gone. He's vapor," Carlson's voice said.

"Find him. Now!" Stan said. He checked the mirrors, looking behind them. He remembered Carlson's brash confidence earlier—the confidence of an agent who had never lost a big one before. Now Carlson sounded contrite. He would be humbled now, another graduate of the Burdett School of Federal Law Enforcement.

A voice in his brain told him that Burdett had wandered away when the agents were watching the game—that it meant nothing, he would reappear in a moment. It was the voice of his old confidence that told him he had thought of everything and his triple-redundant security would do its job. After all, the diamond was sitting in the middle of a bureau motorcade with four heavily armed men within a five-foot radius. Burdett would have to be stupid or crazy—or both—to try anything now, the voice assured him.

It was tempting to listen to that voice. It was

reasonable, perfectly logical. The only problem was that Stan knew it was also completely full of shit.

"He's coming after it," Stan said.

From behind the wheel, Mitch said, "We're fine," but Stan heard the doubt in the agent's own voice.

"I've dealt with this guy before. I don't wanna hear that 'fine' shit."

"Armed caravan. Completely bulletproof. Magnetic locks. Besides, we're nearly there," Mitch replied, gaining confidence as he spoke.

Stan was not convinced. He turned around and took the carry case from between the two security guards who were sitting in the backseat.

"I'm hand-carrying this thing right into the museum," he said. It was a change in the plan, but Stan realized that he had to do *something* differently. His gut was telling him that Burdett was ahead of them, and he had already given Stan one surprise today. Stan would be damned if he let that prick give him another one.

Max walked down a tunnel toward a back entrance of the arena. Every sense was heightened. His ears were noting every sound around him, he could pick out a dozen distinct smells, and everything he saw was brightly colored and in sharp focus. Outwardly calm, he was very alert with a ball of excitement warming him from the inside.

He was on a job and there was nothing else like it. Thinking of Lola, he remembered what they had done last night after their final review of the plan and realized that was not quite true—there was *almost* nothing else like it.

It was different for her, he knew. She was cool under pressure, but she didn't enjoy it the way he did, particularly at times like this when her part was mostly done and she had nothing to do but wait. Even then, she merely coped with the pressure—she didn't live for it.

Max did. There were at least a dozen things he could do well—and he had needed all of those skills just to set up this job—but the job itself was what he did best. There was no doubt in his mind that this was what he was made for.

As he watched the man in the leather jacket approach him, Max felt the comfortable weight of the Lakers Yearbook in his right hand. As they crossed paths, Max casually handed off the Yearbook and the videotape he had placed inside it.

The man in the jacket took it in a smooth movement and Max felt a rush of fresh excitement as he cleared another hurdle. So far, his plan had worked flawlessly, but he didn't let himself think about his final objective. He had a number of tasks to complete. Each one required his total concentration and would get it. Besides, he intended to savor every second of this job.

Outside, Stan had to work to keep the hysteria out of his voice as he shouted into the SUV's radio. "You see him? What's going on?"

"We're looking, we're looking," Carlson said.

Stan scanned the immediate area with his eyes. "Safety's off until they relocate Burdett."

"Stand down. We've got him . . ." Carlson's voice said, a hint of satisfaction in it.

Carlson allowed himself to smile as he looked up at the large screen. "He's still here, on the JumboTron." It was definitely Burdett. He was standing in an aisle with fans all around him. "The fight must've scared him. Probably hid under his seat," Carlson said.

"Burdett doesn't scare easy," Stan's voice responded via the radio. "Get a direct visual."

Carlson took a last look at the JumboTron screen and tried to figure out what section he was seeing. He found a few reference points and brought up his binoculars. Though he found the section quickly, he couldn't find Burdett.

Instinctively, he checked the screen again. Sure enough, Burdett was still there. Carlson raised his binoculars again, a sinking feeling already forming in his chest.

Out on the street, Max pulled out his PDA and read the vehicle identification number that it had just received. He smiled, entered the number, and hit a code he had memorized. A moment later, the FBI Travel Link system logo appeared on the PDA screen. Quickly, he scrolled through a few levels of menu options to confirm what he already knew: every level of control on every instrument in Agent Lloyd's SUV was now available to him.

The Travel Link system had taken weeks for Max to hack into, but in the end the solution had been fairly simple. The Bureau had bought the system from a contractor who produced a number of much simpler computer systems for ordinary consumer cars—systems that monitored basic engine functions and gave drivers maps of where they were going. The contractor's consumer system was very easy to breach, and even though the FBI software was much more sophisticated, it shared a lot of the root computer code with simpler version for the public.

So the FBI had bought a multi-million-dollar house and had never thought to change the locks. He put in his earpiece and clicked another button. "Travel Link activated," a pleasant female voice said.

Stan watched anxiously as the SUV approached the large gate of the museum's security entrance. Finally entering, he should have been relaxed, but his gut was screaming a warning.

"See? We got you here, Stan. No need to panic," Mitch said, the confidence back in his voice.

Stan ignored him and barked into the radio, "Do you have direct visual?"

"Uh . . . not yet," Carlson said, his tone telling Stan

everything he needed to know. Suddenly, he was sure that if a hundred agents took a week to search every inch of the arena, they wouldn't find Burdett.

Looking up, Stan saw a huge banner that read NAPOLEON EXHIBIT OPENING SOON. For a moment, he thought that Burdett had put the sign there to taunt him, but of course that was impossible.

As they pulled up to the security booth, Stan took out his ID. The security officer there took a look and waved them through. Stan could see the museum director and a number of other bigwigs coming out to meet them. Stan knew he should have relaxed then, but he couldn't shake the feeling that something was wrong here—he just couldn't put his finger on it.

The security guards all exited the SUV and then Mitch did as well. Stan took the carry case and got ready to open his own door. Let Burdett try to take the case from him. To do that, he'd have to pry it from Stan's dead fingers.

But before he could pull on the handle to open the door, he heard a click. It made him jump, and then he realized that his door had just locked. Stan looked at the door, confused. Then on instinct he lunged for the driver's side door. It was locked as well.

"What the—" he said.

It was impossible, and yet Stan had no doubt about who was responsible.

"Burdett," he said under his breath, making the word a curse.

Just then, the SUV started by itself. The car went into gear and started reversing back toward the gate.

"What the hell is he doing?" Stan heard Mitch say, and Stan suddenly realized how this looked—like he was taking off with the diamond. As it continued in reverse toward the gate, the two security guards had to leap out of the way. Fighting to brake and then to steer, Stan found that none of the car's controls worked.

The SUV smashed through the gate in reverse and then spun around in the street. For a moment, Stan had to give up fighting with the controls and just hang on. Then the car was going straight again, barreling down the road. Stan continued to wrestle with the wheel, but he knew it was pointless.

Stan knew two things for certain: the first was that Burdett was driving the car; the second was that Stan was screwed.

Chapter Two

From the roof of the warehouse across the street, Max Burdett drove the SUV carrying the diamond, as well as Special Agent Stanley Lloyd. He almost regretted the very public embarrassment this would cause for Lloyd—especially since this was not the first time Max had embarrassed the agent.

As usual, Lloyd was in over his head and his pay grade. There was almost something noble about Lloyd's dogged pursuit of Max, particularly since his success rate over the years remained at a resounding zero. Yet Lloyd kept at it, despite the fact that his past failures had no doubt cost him in his career.

Before actual sympathy crept into his brain, Max reminded himself that if Lloyd had his way, Max would never eat another meal that didn't come from a prison cafeteria. Steering the car toward the warehouse, Max watched as the homeless man walked up to him.

A tense moment passed between the two as they stared at each other. Suddenly, they embraced. The bum pushed Max against the wall, then planted a passionate kiss on his lips.

"Wait!" Max said. "Your beard tickles."

Max saw a latex prosthetic fall to the ground. Then the ragged shirt. At that point, he spared a glance at his partner and said, "Did he tip you?"

"One lousy buck."

"Cheap bastard."

The wig came off next, then the teeth, and in front of him stood the best partner he had ever worked with: Lola Cirillo. She was cool under pressure, and she knew when to stick to a plan and when to improvise. And, of course, she had done things to him that none of his previous partners had ever done.

He gestured to the rest of her clothes with a glance and said, "I'll give you twenty, if you keep stripping."

She smiled and he took in her Latin features, her dark eyes, her dark, straight hair, and her dark skin. Lola was the most beautiful woman he had ever seen, and she was miles away from the fair-skinned girls from home.

They kissed again and he felt the heat immediately. There was an urgency that was stronger than he had ever felt before with a woman. Yes . . . dark hair, eyes, and skin, but inside she was all fire. Just when things were getting interesting, she pulled away and then was all business.

"Ok. Let's do this," she said.

Mitch had watched Stan take off in the SUV in disbelief. He couldn't believe it was happening. He was sure they were safe once they had made it inside the museum gate.

Of course, Stan had still been nervous, but now that Stan was making a play for the diamond himself, it all made sense: he was nervous because he was about to try to steal one of the single most valuable gemstones in the world. There was something strange about the whole mess, but Mitch didn't have time to sort it all out now.

Mitch raced for the nearest SUV and ordered the other agents and guards to do the same. Just as his hand touched the door handle, he heard a loud click that told him the doors had just been locked. Glancing around quickly, he saw that the other men were having the same problem.

All of the Bureau SUVs were locked, apparently by remote. Suddenly, he got a sense of what was really going on here. It didn't make much sense and was ballsy even for Max Burdett, yet it fit the facts.

There was no more time to waste, Mitch realized, so he did the only thing he could do. He started after Stan's SUV at a dead run, gesturing for the other agents to follow.

* * *

The car made a sharp left turn that tossed Stan back toward the passenger seat. Then a right turn that banged his head into the driver's side window. Finally, to add insult to injury, the radio blasted a loud disco song at full volume. The wipers came on at nearly the same time, and Stan was suddenly sure that Burdett was messing with him.

Well, this game would end soon enough, and Stan was determined to give Burdett at least one good surprise today. He looked forward to that moment—when he could once and for all wipe that smug grin off of Max Burdett's face.

Then the two front air bags deployed. One caught him in the face and chest, popping open at more than one hundred and fifty miles an hour and throwing him back against the seat.

A second later, the SUV screeched to a halt and Stan heard a heavy door slam down behind him. When the disorientation from the air bag impact began to clear, Stan realized that, wherever they were, it was pitch-black.

Thankfully, the radio was off now and the only sound Stan heard was the sound of his own heavy breathing. He clutched the diamond case with one hand and drew his gun with the other. Despite his successes so far, Burdett had a long way to go before he could get his hands on the diamond itself.

And to do that, he would have to go through Stan first.

Fortunately, the air bags had immediately deflated, and Stan was free to move around in the SUV again. He scanned all the windows, looking for any movement in the darkness. Whatever he did, Burdett would have to move fast, because the Bureau would be able to use the vehicle's GPS locator to find it quickly.

Just then, he heard a voice in his headset. It was Mitch. "Stan. Stan, we've got a problem."

"Yeah, I kinda figured that out . . . I was just hurtled into darkness in a car I can't control!"

In the police holding area of the Staples Center arena was the drunk fan who had caused such a ruckus during the game. "Let me outta here. I want outta here," he said in an accent that was pure East L.A.

The cops milling around ignored him, as did the other detainee who sat on a bench behind him—a young man who sat dejectedly in his seat.

The drunken fan watched with interest as two policemen reviewed a game tape on one of the security monitors.

"He was definitely there at some point," one of the policemen said.

"I want my lawyer," the drunk fan interjected. The police ignored him again, and then he was suddenly quiet and, apparently, sober. He turned to the other detainee and said with a very distinct Irish brogue, "Do you have a smoke, mate?"

Bright lights flashed on outside somewhere for a few seconds. Stan was temporarily blinded. After a few seconds, his vision cleared and he saw two figures in black masks approaching him. One of them was male, about six feet tall. The other was female—very female—about five-two. Stan knew exactly who they were and raised his gun without hesitation.

Regulations, training, and common sense told Stan that it was foolish to fire a weapon inside a closed vehicle. There was the obvious danger of flying glass, not to mention the hell the blast would do to your hearing. And since Stan used a big nine-millimeter—affectionately known as "the cannon" around the Bureau—these dangers were all significantly increased.

Stan didn't waste a second thinking about the dangers. He took aim at Burdett and fired. The report in the closed car was damned loud but to his surprise, didn't have any effect on the windshield, which didn't even crack, let alone shatter.

Cursing himself for an idiot, he muttered, "Bulletproofed. Damn." He'd forgotten that these new security vehicles were heavily reinforced. Well, it wasn't the first mistake he'd made today.

As this sank in, there was a loud crack outside and the blinding flash of a magnesium concussion grenade going off in front of the car. Stan knew the grenades well because they were part of the Bureau's arsenal, particularly useful in raids or other situations where agents were facing a number of armed hostiles. The grenades could immediately stun and blind suspects.

Though he had used them against perps a number of times in the past, he had never been on the receiving end of a blast. Now that he was, he saw they were damned effective.

* * *

Max went to work immediately. Lola handed him a screwdriver and he used it to reach the latch that opened the hood. It took him only a second and Lola had the hood up as soon as it clicked.

He handed her a hose that she placed into the air-conditioning system. They had rehearsed this series of movements on an identical model car dozens of times, but in the heat of the job Burdett was sure they were beating their best time by a significant margin.

It always happened—the adrenaline pumped, the senses sharpened, the clarity descended. He loved this work and Lola was the best he had ever seen beside himself. He decided to have some fun with her.

"Have you decided? Mediterranean, India, or Caribbean?" he teased.

Lola rose to the bait immediately. "Isn't there a better time to talk about this?"

Max shrugged. "I can't think of one. A few more seconds and he'll be out." It was true: this job was nearly over. *This last job,* his mind supplied.

It was a fact: with this last job accomplished, there would be no need to ever pull another one. There would be nothing to prove, and money certainly would never be a problem, even if they lived as well as he'd planned.

"Max, how about Mexico?" Lola asked.

"Can't take the water," he replied.

"What about Paris?"

"Can't take the French." Max leaned over to steal a quick kiss.

Lola, disengaging, looked Max in the eyes and said, "Max, promise me paradise."

"You got it," he replied. "Can we talk about this after we gas agent Lloyd?"

"Sure thing, honey."

Max took an industrial syringe from Lola and injected the black liquid into the hose, and, thus, the ventilation system. Lloyd would be out for a while and awake with a splitting headache. He would also be plenty angry, but that was nothing new.

The job was nearly finished. All that remained now was to collect the prize.

Black gas seeped into the car through the vents. Lloyd had recovered from effects of the grenade and saw the gas almost immediately. He fought desperately to close the vents. When that failed he held his hands over them. Finally, he put his shirt over his mouth as he coughed and choked for air.

Lloyd was about Max's age, with close-cropped, thinning blond hair. He lacked the polish of most agents and his rough-and-tumble look made him seem out of place in the FBI.

Max watched tensely, sorry to see Lloyd's final moments of defeat. That defeat and plenty of regret were written all over Lloyd's face. The agent knew this battle was lost and had no doubt realized that another loss at Max's hands would be the final nail in the coffin that was his career. Max was suddenly glad that this was his last job.

Max liked the game, and he only played to win, but he had never seen the moment of his foe's defeat so clearly before. Tempted to look away, Max forced himself to watch and leaned forward to make sure there were no surprises. Lloyd began listing to the side. He was starting to pass out. There were only seconds left now, if that. Max looked at his watch. "A few seconds and he'll be . . ."

Max didn't get to complete the thought. In a surprisingly quick movement, Lloyd brought his gun to bear, pointing it at the air vent and firing in a single movement. The action must have taken a remarkable act of will, though what happened next Max realized owed quite a bit to luck.

As the end of the gun flared, Max saw the trajectory of the bullet in his mind even before his chest exploded in pain. He flew backward, as if hit by a sledgehammer instead of a few grams of steel. As he hit the ground, Burdett realized that he might have been better off if he had been hit by a sledgehammer.

He hit the ground hard and looked down at the wound. Blood was running freely.

"Max!" Lola cried out, rushing to his side.

Max had realized long ago that, in his business, he would likely get only one mistake. Well, he had planned this job to the last detail and had never considered that the vents could make them vulnerable. He cursed himself. It might just as easily have been Lola as him, and it might not have been in the shoulder.

"Shit!" Lola exclaimed from above him. Then she knelt down beside him, pulling off his mask. "Max . . . Max," she said. There was concern in her voice, and Burdett felt woozy, his eyes dropping closed. "Max! Look at me. Look at me!" Lola yelled, slapping him hard across the face.

Fighting the crushing pain, Max forced his bloody lips

into a thin smile. "Paradise," he whispered to Lola, who was hunched over his prone body, clearly alarmed by his condition.

"Don't worry," he said. "Get the rock." She leaned him against a wall and rushed back to the SUV.

As he waited, Max thought he felt the bleeding slow down, though it hadn't stopped. He applied pressure with his good hand. It hurt like hell. In his entire career, he had never worked with a gun. Before, he had said that guns were simply bad form, amateurish, but the truth was that they made him nervous and he simply didn't like them.

And this was all *before* he had gotten shot.

Lola was back after only a few seconds and she was holding the black carry case. In spite of the pain in his shoulder, he felt a rush of excitement. They had done it. The diamond was theirs. Max found himself smiling and looking forward to their celebration.

A twinge from his shoulder told him that they might have to forgo their usual celebration ritual while they got his shoulder taken care of. He reminded himself that the job wasn't over until they had gotten away clean, and the gunshot wound made things much tougher. It was a new wrinkle, and a serious one. He couldn't go to a regular hospital, because by law hospitals had to report gunshot wounds, and the FBI would be on his tail in minutes.

It was a problem—an interesting one in its way—and would require some improvisation, but Max's mind was already coming up with answers. He could make a few calls to get what they needed. There were always places to go to get things like this taken care of quietly, particularly if money was no object.

He felt a moment of dizziness and realized they didn't have a lot of time. Lola wouldn't be able to carry him. They needed to get to the car immediately. Quickening his pace in spite of his body's protest, Burdett hurried for the car waiting only a few feet away.

Once she had him seated in the passenger seat, Lola took her cell phone out immediately. Max felt his head swimming and knew that he wouldn't be much help for the rest of this operation, but that was okay. He trusted his partner.

Since he was leading the way, Mitch was the first to see the SUV slowly hiccupping down the street, limping back toward them. He stopped running and heard the other agents slow down behind him.

Less than a minute later, the vehicle came to a stop right in front of them. Mitch knew immediately what had happened. Stan was sitting in the front seat, still wearing a seatbelt, but he was unconscious.

Mitch signaled for the other agents to surround the SUV and took a position by the driver's side door. Wary of another trick, he waited for a moment and saw that Stan was starting to come to. Mitch opened the driver's side door as three other agents opened the other three doors.

Stan looked up at him, confused and disoriented, though to Mitch's surprise he was still clutching the black carry case. It was unopened, so there was still hope. The museum director brushed passed Mitch and leaned down to grab the case. He produced a key card and inserted it into the case. The lid immediately popped open.

The diamond was not inside.

For a second, Mitch's mind rejected what actually *was* inside the case. It didn't compute and seemed like a bad joke: nestled into the space where the diamond belonged was a crumpled one-dollar bill. Mitch recognized it immediately. It was the bill Stan had given him to give to the homeless window washer.

Burdett woke up in a room he didn't recognize. His first thought was that it was a hospital. It had a spare, industrial look that for a moment made him think it was a prison hospital. Then Lola's face slowly drifted into focus in front of him.

She was smiling and that told him everything he needed to know. Well, almost everything. "Where?" he asked, his mouth feeling like it was full of marbles and cotton.

"A small clinic in East L.A.," Lola said. Then she was holding up something. It took several seconds before his eyes could focus on the small object in her hand. It was flattened out, but there was no mistaking the bullet. "A souvenir," she said.

"You were lucky," a second voice said. "The bullet just missed the sub-clavin artery. And there was no bone trauma or permanent muscle damage. Some of my best work, if I do say so myself."

Burdett saw that the person who spoke was a remarkably clean-cut young man . . . his doctor. "Thank you," Burdett said. For a moment Burdett wondered how a man like that ended up in these shabby surroundings, doing this kind of work. Well, there were a lot of paths to places like this, and Burdett knew better than to ask questions of a surgeon who was taking care of him on the sly—and who was risking prison for accepting money not to report the incident.

"However," the doctor added, "You were hit in the pectoralis muscles. As the bullet entered, it damaged what's called the brachial plexis. That's a grouping of nerves right here," the doctor said pointing to the area between his shoulder and upper chest. "The bullet grazed some of the nerves so you will see some loss of fine motor movement and maybe a loss of sensation in the arm and/or hand."

Max felt himself become suddenly more alert, and more than a little concerned. "Nerve damage. Is it permanent?"

The doctor shook his head. "These are peripheral nerves, which means they can regenerate over time. You will improve, but it's impossible to predict how much."

Max shook his head, relieved. In his business, he needed to be a hundred percent. *But this is your last job,* a voice in his head said. Max recognized that voice as Lola's.

"I need to get out of here," Burdett said.

The doctor shook his head. "You just came out of surgery. If nothing else, you need another few hours to recover from the anesthetic. Plus, I'd like to watch you for—"

"No," Burdett said. "We're not safe here. And you're not safe if we're found."

The doctor looked at Lola, who nodded her head. Still, the doctor took a few moments to think it over.

"Okay, I'll give you a mild stimulant to get you on your feet." Then he turned to Lola. "You will have to change the dressing on the wound every day for the next ten. Then the stitches will have to come out. That you can do yourself if you're not squeamish. I'll give you antibiotics. Make sure he follows the instructions and takes them all. I'll also give you something he can take for the pain for the next day or two."

Lola nodded again and the doctor gave Burdett something directly into the IV tube. In a surprisingly short time, Burdett felt his head clear, and his body felt like his own again. The doctor watched him and said, "For a little while, you're going to feel like you're in much better shape than you're actually in. Don't overdo it. Like I said, that's some of my best work—don't mess it up." Then he turned to Lola again. "Get him into bed quickly and let him sleep."

Max got to his feet and the doctor took out the IV quickly. He put Max's arm in a sling. Lola helped him dress, and the doctor led him through the darkened clinic. Burdett looked at the clock. It was nearly midnight. He had been out for a while. They thanked the doctor and made their way through a back door.

Out in the night, the cool air helped revive him even more. After they got into the car, Lola said. "We could stay local. It's a big city."

Burdett shook his head. "No, we'll stick to the plan."

It was late, so traffic was fine and they made it out of L.A. quickly. In less than an hour they were in Anaheim. Disneyland had been Lola's idea, and it was a good one. Stan wouldn't think to look for them there.

They got to the room quickly. It was just in time: Burdett could feel the drugs start to wear off. Sitting on the bed, he waited as Lola dug into a small duffel bag and pulled out a black pouch made of felt. Reaching inside, she pulled out the diamond and handed it to him.

He held it in his hands. It was cool to the touch. Though he had seen one of its sister stones, he was still amazed at the sight. After millions of years deep in the earth, it had been found through dumb luck. At fifty-eight carats, it was one of the largest gem-quality cut diamonds in the world. But most amazing was that it was completely flawless and had perfect D color—meaning it was completely clear. Gem-quality diamonds larger than a few carats were astonishingly rare. At this size they were almost unheard of.

Diamonds that large usually had massive internal fractures. In fact, all of the Napoleon diamonds, of which this was one, had started out at more than one hundred and fifty carats before they had been cut. Master jewelers had studied each stone for years, looking at its fracture lines, inclusions, and crystalline structures. And even after all that work, a stone could shatter even when a master made the first strike with a chisel.

Well, this diamond and two more like it had survived the process and had been placed into the sword Napoleon wore on the day of his wedding to Josephine. It was said that he then kept the diamond-encrusted sword with him as a talisman—only losing it at Waterloo.

In his hands, Burdett was holding the unlikely combination of nature, luck, fate, and craft. Its very existence was a miracle. And it was his. His and Lola's. It was the culmination of their life's work. It was also their future.

"Okay, you need to sleep," Lola said, starting to pull off his slacks. There it was, that accent of hers, the musical tone of her voice: exotic and full of promise—and just for him.

"Not yet, we still haven't celebrated properly," he said, eyeing her seriously.

"Oh, no. In your condition, it might kill you," she said, disbelief in her eyes.

"Let's find out," he said.

It hadn't killed him and had been a little tricky with one hand. Not his best work, but under the circumstances Burdett was pretty pleased with himself.

When Burdett woke, it was daylight. He checked the clock and saw that it was four p.m. His shoulder was sore, but not as bad as he had feared. His head was clear, except for a slight grogginess and a headache— no worse than he felt after a night with a few too many cocktails. Altogether, not a bad trade for the diamond.

Lola came out of the bathroom wearing a towel.

"Ummmm," he said, seeing her.

She smiled and shook her head. "Don't get any more ideas," she said.

"I'm always thinking three steps ahead," he said. "It's the nature of my work."

"Well, let's think about changing your bandages," she said.

"Later. I need a shower," he said. He got out of bed

and fought off Lola's insistence that she help him, and he changed the bandages himself. By now the pain in his shoulder was a dull roar and he took one of the doctor's pain pills.

When he was out he saw that Lola was dressed. She was wearing the yellow dress with red flowers and his favorite perfume. Leaning into the mirror, she was putting on her earrings. He watched her for a moment and found his breath catch in his throat, as it often did when he came upon her doing something mundane.

"Whatever you're thinking, forget it," she said. She glanced at him through the mirror, a smile on her face.

"I was just going to ask you a question," he said.

She shook her head and said, "I think you need a little more rest." Her tone was still playful but firm.

What he said next he said with dead seriousness. "Marry me."

She was still smiling when she said, "What?"

"I said marry me, Lola," he replied.

She glanced at him through the mirror again, and then turned to look at his face directly. She read his expression, saw that he was serious.

"Marry me," he repeated. He could see her forming another question in her mind. *Are you serious?* She was about to ask, but saw something in his face that gave her her answer first.

Burdett found that he had never been more serious about anything in his life. She looked at him and he could see that he had genuinely surprised her, which he'd never really done before. As a result, the look on her face was something he had never seen before. She was stunned. He knew how she felt—he was more than a little surprised himself.

Her mouth opened and for a long moment she didn't speak.

"Of course, if you would like some time to think about it . . ." he began.

There it was, the smile. Her face lit up and gave him all the answer he needed. Then she was leaning into him, her soft lips on his own.

When she finally pulled away, she looked at him and said, "What did that doctor give you and what are we going to do when it wears off?"

He smiled back and said, "I don't think it will wear off. I think the condition may be permanent."

They decided on room service after all.

The next morning when Burdett woke up, he found that Lola had already been up for a while and had packed everything they needed. He got ready quickly and they were at the airport in plenty of time. By noon, they were on the plane and in the air. Burdett let himself relax the final notch.

The job really was over now. *Not just the job,* his mind supplied, *the career.*

That would take some getting used to.

The flight attendant came by with their drinks. When Burdett took his, she asked, "Honeymoon?"

"Vacation," Max said, at the same moment that Lola said, "Retirement."

"A bit of everything," Max added, looking out the window. The sun was setting in a brilliant show of reds and oranges.

Chapter Three

After the first week on Paradise Island, Burdett was able to throw away the sling. A few days later the bandage came off and then the stitches came out. By then, Burdett found himself actually relaxing on the beach as he tried to get full motion and strength back in his hand and arm. It was slow, but he had nothing but time.

The beach house was very comfortable, the Caribbean sea amazing, and the private beach allowing them plenty of time for relaxation. In fact, Burdett realized they had never *relaxed* more often or more energetically. If this was retirement, he was all for it. They walked the beach, explored the island, explored each other. At the end of the second week, as they sat on the small porch, Burdett realized that this was officially the longest vacation he had ever taken in his life.

No, not a vacation. This is my life now, he realized.

"I could do this forever," Lola said, almost as if she had been reading his mind.

"That's the plan," Burdett replied.

"What about tonight, want to go dancing at that little tiki bar?" Lola asked.

An image of Lola moving to the rhythm of a Junkanoo band crossed his mind and he said yes quicker than he'd meant to, which made her smile. He was glad for the smile. For the first few days, she had hovered over him and checked his shoulder every day. She hadn't been able to relax or leave his side for more than a few minutes.

Now that the stitches were out and the money from the diamond safely tucked into their bank account— their *joint* bank account—she seemed to stop worrying. That night they had had a light dinner at the bar and danced. The band was good and Lola looked wonderful on the floor.

Lola put her hands on his shoulders and maneuvered him backward. There was a twinkle in her eye and he saw that she was up to something. Burdett felt himself bump lightly into someone behind him. She turned him around and bumped herself into a tourist wearing a loud sport coat. Almost too quick for his eye to follow, Lola's hand reached into one of the man's jacket pockets. She brought it tight to her chest and smiled up at him.

Raising his eyebrows, Burdett said, "Show-off."

"I'm not keeping it, just playing," she said.

Burdett spun her back near the tourist couple and she bumped again into the man. There was a flash of movement and a moment later she didn't have the wallet anymore.

"I wrote my vows. You?" she said, looking up at him expectantly.

"Work in progress," Max replied.

"Let me hear what you have so far?" she asked.

"Let's wait. It's more romantic," Burdett said.

"Maybe I should help you. Remind you of how fantastic I am," she said, pulling herself closer to him.

Burdett shook his head. "I don't need reminding."

She lowered her voice, looking right into his eyes, and said, "And of all the things you want to do for me the rest of our lives. I have a wish list, you know."

"How am I doing so far?" he asked.

"Not bad," she said.

There was frantic movement nearby and Burdett turned to see the tourist in the sport coat frantically searching for his wallet. Finally, he pulled it out of a pocket and looked at it strangely. Burdett realized that Lola had intentionally put it back in a different pocket. They looked at each other and laughed.

He saw something else in her eyes when he looked at her, something he recognized. It was time to head back to the beach house. Burdett wouldn't let a look like that go unanswered. He had never been one to procrastinate, not in work and not in these matters.

Then why haven't you written your vows? A voice

inside asked him. Burdett brushed the thought aside. They were still on vacation, figuring out their new life. There was plenty of time for vows, and for anything else they wanted to do.

The next day they rode horses through the forest and on the beach, took the boat out, though *boat* was not nearly a big enough word for it. It was a Riva, very sleek and very fast. Riva was an Italian company that dated back to the late 1800s. It was a legend today, making some of the finest yachts in the world.

Burdett remembered his father talking about seeing Rivas when he was in the navy. It was one of the few stories from his brief navy years that Burdett's father told. "If I ever get rich, I'll have one of those," his father had said. It would have taken many years of his Irish father's postman's salary to pay for one, Burdett realized. As a child, Burdett had thought he would someday buy his dad his boat, but his father had died before that had been possible.

Now Burdett had succeeded beyond his own childish dreams of fortune. Yet his father had lived only to see the very beginning of Burdett's career, which had been full of false starts and petty trouble.

"What are you thinking?" Lola said, reaching around from behind to hug him while he manned the wheel.

"Nothing," Burdett said. Then he reached down for the throttle and said, "Why don't we open her up." He hit the throttle and the Riva shot forward, skimming the waves, seeming to barely touch the water.

Lola squealed and hugged him tighter.

That night, Lola disappeared into the bathroom.

When Burdett finally went to look for her, he found her in the tub, bubbles all around her, the room lit by candles. He didn't need an engraved invitation and joined her quickly.

Something smelled familiar. He looked around and picked up a bottle of bath oil and sniffed it. "Ah, Morocco," he said.

"They're the same bubbles from Madame Casoon's bathroom. Remember?"

Burdett smiled. "Yeah. I remember the sapphires. Two hundred and thirty carats' worth." It hadn't been a bad night's work.

"Perfectly cut. Blue as the Côte d'Azur. Protected by a two-wire alarm . . ."

Burdett finished for her: ". . . And that flimsy safe with the G-rated TLTR-30 doors and granulated tungsten carbide hard plates."

"As if that would stop *us*," she said.

They both laughed at that. Madame Casoon didn't deserve the stones. She certainly didn't bother to take the precautions necessary to make sure she kept them. And she certainly never wore them. As far as Burdett was concerned, he and Lola had liberated the jewels.

"We were two hours late getting out. Jumping into her tub was the least professional thing we ever did," he said.

"But it was fun," Lola protested.

"We just missed the maid showing up for work—" Burdett began.

"—to a wet tub and a blown safe," Lola finished for him.

Burdett smiled. "It was worth the risk," he said.

"It was a hell of a first date," Lola said.

That was true. It had been their first official date, their first successful job together, and their first after-job celebration. Burdett pulled her closer.

"I know what you're doing. Don't even try it, Max," she said, a hint of teasing in her voice.

"Just trying to keep the memories alive," he said.

Lola's hands stroked his arms up to his shoulders and found the bullet scar there. It was still red, angry. The skin had healed but it still looked alien to him, as if it wasn't really part of his body.

"Then how come we never talk about *this*?" Lola asked, her face suddenly serious.

Max felt himself tense. "I don't want to talk about it. I'd rather forget it," he said.

"Well I can't. Three inches to the right and I'm alone. While you were getting stitched up, I saw my life without you."

Max smiled. "But I'm still here."

Lola's face didn't soften a bit. "Yes you are. We need to make new memories . . . different ones. I'm glad we're done."

Max glanced down at the scar. Angry. Red. It taunted him with his failure, the angle he'd missed, the possibility he'd overlooked. It still bothered Lola that he had been shot and could have died, but what woke him up in a cold sweat in the middle of the night was the thought that it might just as easily have been her.

* * *

Max stood at the tiki bar, waiting for Lola. It was late in the day, his favorite time. The faint sound of reggae music floated over the perfect white sand where tanned bodies soaked in the sun. For them, this place was a paradise where they would spend a few days— a week or two at most. And that whole time they would dream of never leaving.

The men might dream of spending their time with a woman like Lola, or Lola herself if they had seen her on the beach. In their six months on the island, Max had lived that life, the life they dreamed about, the exotic life he had dreamed about since he was a boy who wanted to get away from a life so ordinary, so familiar that it was numbing, deadening.

In his months here, Max had gotten quite a tan himself, no small feat for a white boy from Ireland. He'd also bought himself his first pair of honest-to-God Bermuda shorts. It was a good life, he had to admit. Certainly nothing to complain about.

But it's nothing like being on a job, his mind supplied. There was nothing even remotely like the feeling he had when he was planning and executing a job.

Max shrugged off the thought. Well, he knew that retirement would take some getting used to. His own father had not lived to retire. Well, he'd never stopped working at any rate. But the fact was that his father had retired in virtually every way that really mattered when Max was very young. But his father's retirement wasn't on a pristine beach with an exotic beauty. His retirement had been to an easy chair in front of a television set. No exotic drinks for him, just pint after pint. Numbness and silence. Then he would pass out, wake up later to stagger up to bed, go to work the next day, and do it again.

As a result, Max could never stomach dark Guinness.

He looked at the tropical drink menu, though he had learned it by heart months ago. "Luc, what's in the Caribbean Romance again?"

Luc was sticking umbrellas in the various fruity cocktails on the bar. Max liked Luc. He was a good-looking young man, an American who had worked at the tiki bar since they had arrived. He was also part of the fantasy for many of the single women who came to the island, and as far as Max could tell, Luc, God bless him, did his best not to disappoint them.

"Light rum, amaretto, orange juice, pineapple juice, splash of grenadine," Luc said.

"What about the Pink Paradise?"

"Coconut rum, amaretto, cranberry juice, pineapple juice, and orange juice," Luc said.

"People actually drink the stuff?" Max asked.

Luc smiled. "They love it. It makes 'em feel exotic," Luc said.

Well, who was Max to begrudge them their few days of fantasy, when he lived it month in and month out?

"Give me a Jack on the rocks. It doesn't have a fancy name, but if it was good enough for Frank, it's good enough for me."

"Frank?" Luc said.

Max raised his eyebrows. "Sinatra," he said.

Luc poured, holding up a little paper umbrella. "Did Frank take an umbrella?"

"Not even when it rained," Max said, taking his

drink and heading for a chair overlooking the water. For the thousandth time he thought how beautiful, how perfect. This place, this moment was more than any man could want, yet something rose up in his chest as it had done lately when he looked out on the perfection.

He knew the feeling well. He had felt the same thing looking at the diamond just a few days after they had arrived. The job, of course, had been a rush, as was holding the diamond the first time—seeing its own perfection, possessing it. The feeling had lasted a day, maybe two. On the third day, it was time to make the transfer to the new owner and Max had not even been sad to see it go.

The feeling of *getting* the diamond was something he knew he would remember for the rest of his life. And *possessing* it that first time had been something. Getting meant something to him. Possessing meant something. But keeping . . .

He realized long ago that he was not built for it. It simply held no allure for him. Of course, in the past he had always thought that a big enough job would satisfy him; a big enough payout would be enough. That, in the end, he could be satisfied.

But what if enough wasn't enough?

And where did that leave him? There was no point in doing the one thing he was meant to do. His work had already made him wealthy. And on the last job it had nearly killed him. It could have just as easily killed Lola.

I saw my life without you, Lola had said to him. He didn't have to think very hard to imagine his life without her. In fact, no imagination was required at all; he

45

simply had to think of any day of his childhood, thinking about his father living in his chair, living without his wife, Max's mother.

Max barely remembered his mother; he was too young when she died. What he remembered most was the change in his father. Perhaps Max wasn't built to understand *keeping*, but he certainly understood *losing*.

After ten minutes, or an hour, Max saw a motorized rubber raft, a Zodiac, approach the shore. He recognized Lola from a distance. She was with her dive guide. He was young, and handsome, but Lola had never given him any reason to worry. When the boat reached the shore, the guide helped her off the boat and then she approached Max.

"How was it?" Max asked.

"Amazing. You'd love it. The only sounds are your breath, your heartbeat. Just like a job. And the reef is like a thousand jewels sparkling in front of you. But you can't take 'em, no matter how much you want to. You should come next time," she said.

Her girlish enthusiasm touched something in him, but he shook his head and said, "I'll stay where I can breathe unassisted, thanks."

They had lunch at the bar and then Max and Lola got into his 1968 Chevy Camaro convertible. It had a turbo 350-cubic-inch engine with four-barrel carburetor and dual exhaust and was in better condition than most of the top show cars of the same year and model. When Max had bought it, it was all original, though he had not been able to resist a few upgrades, including a Holley carburetor and a hydraulic cam with crane roller rockers, and of course a state-of-the-art sound system.

As a result it was likely the fastest car on the island. Of course, the comparison was hardly fair. Most of the cars on the island were small, practical fuel-efficient cars like the ones in Europe, like the ones he had seen growing up. Well, there was nothing practical about the Camaro. That thought made him smile and he floored the gas.

He could sense Lola's smile and had her at her tennis lesson in a few minutes. For Lola, tennis was another new passion. She took to things quickly, throwing herself into them with gusto. An hour later, he returned to see her still on the court. Nick was the local tennis pro— young and handsome. *Another one,* Max thought.

At the moment, young and handsome Nick was standing behind Lola, his hands on her waist as he moved her hips through a simulated forehand.

As Max got out of the car he heard Nick say, "There. Follow through high towards the fence."

"Careful," Lola said to Nick. "My fiancé."

Nick reflexively took a step back. When Max reached the edge of the court he said, "The hands-on approach, huh?"

After an embarrassed smile, Nick replied, "It's the personal touch that gets the results."

"Max," Lola said, her tone making it both a warning and a request.

"Do you play?" Nick asked.

"I have," Max replied.

"Then come on, grip it and rip it," Nick said. There it was, the challenge. Max had put him on the spot with the "hands-on" comment. Young Nick was determined to get some of his own back.

Well, he was young enough not to know any better.

He had to fight the urge to teach the cocky tennis pro a lesson. Taking another look at the smirk on Nick's face, Max decided not to fight the urge after all.

Leaning down, Max took a racquet from Nick's bag, taking care to choose one of the mediocre ones. He gripped it a bit awkwardly in his left hand.

Nick hit the ball to him from across the court, being easy on him. Max managed a feeble return. "You should sign up for a series. I could really help you," Nick said, his tone full of friendly condescension.

Max shrugged affably and said, "How's this? We'll play. If you win, you get my car. If I win, you give Lola free lessons for the rest of the year . . . from across the net."

Nick smirked, the smile of the young and about-to-be-taken. "Okay, serve 'em up," he said, tossing Max the ball.

Max caught the ball and switched the racquet to his right hand. Max enjoyed the look of confusion on the young man's face. Up until now, Nick had thought he would show up the dumb tourist in front of his fiancée. More or less harmless fun, and Max was only too happy to play along, to a point.

But once the game started, Max knew only one way to play: to win. He tossed the ball into the air and put the serve just where he wanted it—and just out of Nick's reach. The young man looked stunned.

"He's right-handed?" Nick asked.

"I told you to be careful," Lola said.

To his credit, Nick had been a pretty gracious loser. In fact, he'd even offered to give Lola her first free lesson immediately.

A figure dressed in black approached the beach house. He had come prepared to have to work for this, but in the end he hadn't needed any of his locksmith tools. The simplest tool in his arsenal, a screwdriver, had been all he needed to jimmy the shutter that covered the open window. All it had cost him was a torn shirt as he climbed through the window.

For a thief who had penetrated some of the tightest security in the world, Burdett was very sloppy with his own home security. Climbing into the window, the figure closed the shutter carefully behind him. He took in the living room: everything in it was expensive, but then again Burdett could afford it many times over, which might explain why he didn't bother with security.

The figure passed some kind of game board with black and white stones layed out as if someone was in mid-game. It was an exotic game, foreign. Then he remembered: it was a go board, from Japan—a fancy-ass version of checkers, as near as he could tell. Then the figure saw an easel, as well as a number of canvasses and paints, and some half-finished paintings of people. The artist was working in oil—obvious from the telltale smell of turpentine.

Moving slowly through the room, the figure passed photos of Burdett and his girlfriend. On a table by the

DVD player, he saw a DVD marked TWO-DAY RENTAL. Picking it up, the figure caught the title and almost laughed out loud. It read: *To Catch a Thief*.

In the kitchen, he looked quickly through the drawers. Then he found something interesting at the wet bar, a nearly full bottle of Johnnie Walker Blue. It wasn't exactly what he was looking for, but it would certainly hit the spot. Reaching up onto a nearby shelf, the figure grabbed a glass. As he did, he felt his shirt pull up to reveal the nine-millimeter automatic he had holstered at his side.

Chapter Four

It was getting late in the day; the sun was not as strong and the wind was kicking up just a little. It was Max's favorite time to be out in the convertible. His only regret that the damn island wasn't big enough for him to really open up the Camaro for long.

Too quickly, they approached the house. For a second, he felt a flash of warning. He had always had good instincts and had refined them on countless jobs. Max didn't question them now. For a moment, he was glad that Lola was still at her lesson.

As he approached the door, Max's eyes were drawn to the ground in front of one of the shutters. Someone had been there, he was sure of it. Then he saw it: the shutter on one of the windows was slightly scraped.

Moving quickly, Max walked around to the side of the house and the small shed there. Unlocking the door, he reached up and brought out a paint can, popped it open, and pulled out a snub-nosed thirty-eight. He didn't like guns and he never brought one on a job, but this was his home, his and Lola's.

Quietly, Max entered through the front door, and then slipped into the living room through the French doors. His gun was out and pointed at the intruder before he had consciously registered the man's presence. "State your business," Max barked. Then he realized that he knew the man who was now lounging in a chair in his living room.

Special Agent Stanley Lloyd had a glass of Max's best whiskey in his hand, the bottle next to him on the table. Lloyd barely looked up at Max as he casually thumbed through a book of snapshots—photos of him and Lola. Max felt a rush of anger at the invasion. It must have shown on his face, because Lloyd was suddenly alert and said, "You gonna shoot an FBI agent, Burdett?"

Max considered the question seriously as Lloyd drew his own nine-millimeter. "All I see is an intruder," Max said. Lloyd took a big sip of his drink. "One who just swallowed eighty dollars' worth of my best whiskey," he added.

Lloyd eyed the glass for a moment and said, "There are those who say the expensive stuff is no better than shelf whiskey. Those are the poor folks." Then Lloyd drained his glass. Without looking at him, Lloyd said,

"Put down the weapon. Don't make me shoot you again."

Max exhaled sharply and through force of will put a lid on his anger and lowered his gun. "Again?" Max said, with mock innocence.

"Is that the way we're gonna play it?" Lloyd asked.

Max didn't want to play this game at all, or any game with this man. "What are you doing in my house, Agent Lloyd?"

"Sitting, drinking, eating chocolate," Lloyd said.

"You got a warrant?" Max asked.

Shaking his head, Lloyd said, "FBI doesn't have jurisdiction here."

Max nodded. "I know, that's why I came here."

"I don't think it is," Stan said, slapping down a color brochure in front of Max. The brochure advertised a fancy cruise ship called the *Seven Seas Navigator* and its "Diamond Voyage." Max recognized the ship. In fact, he could have told Lloyd its metric tonnage, total water displacement, and the last time the security system had been serviced.

"I don't cruise," was all he said, his voice and face betraying nothing.

"Too good for shuffleboard, huh?" Lloyd said, an insufferable smirk on his face.

When Max didn't respond, Lloyd opened up the brochure and held it up. "The *Seven Seas Navigator*. Docking here for a solid week. They're having a nice promotion for the maiden voyage. Calling it the Diamond Voyage. A gem exhibit whose star attraction is: the third Napoleon diamond. Stop me when I get to the part you don't know."

Max looked at the brochure. There was a portrait of Napoleon holding his sword, three large diamonds laid into the hilt. Underneath it, there was a modern photo of the third diamond on a velvet display. "It's the only one you haven't stolen," Lloyd said.

"Allegedly," Max said, keeping his tone light.

"It's worth, what, thirty-two million?" Lloyd asked.

Max couldn't resist and said, "Thirty-five, at Sotheby's. A fence would give you twenty."

"Steep markdown," Lloyd said.

Max gave a small shrug and said, "But it'd be a clean twenty."

Watching him closely, Lloyd said, "And it's going to be right here for a whole week. The last of the set. And I suspect you plan to purloin it."

Max was impressed for a moment and said, "*Purloin?* You learn that at Quantico?"

Shaking his head, Lloyd said, "Crossword puzzles. Since I lost Napoleon two I spend a lot of time by myself."

"Is that so? Well, I don't," Max said. He thought of Lola and realized that he definitely didn't want Lloyd here when she returned. "So finish your drink and get out."

Offended, Lloyd stood up. "Just because you're English doesn't mean you need to hide your emotions."

Max had had it. The game, the charade, was over. "I'm Irish. We let you know how we feel—get the fuck out." With a smirk, Lloyd slapped the brochure into Max's chest, then turned around and retrieved something from the chair: the black carry case from the heist.

"And you can take any bugs you planted along with you. I'm retired."

Suddenly, Lloyd's face was the model of innocence. "Bugs?"

"Four letter word for 'electronic surveillance device,'" Max said.

"A retired guy wouldn't have anything to worry about from those," Lloyd said as he headed for the door. He hesitated near the television and picked up the copy of *To Catch a Thief*. "Mind if I borrow this?" he asked.

"Take it. You might learn something," he said. As Lloyd turned for the door again, Max noticed something and said, "Is that my shirt?"

"Yeah," Lloyd said, unapologetically. "Mine got a little pitted. Hope you don't mind."

Then Agent Lloyd was out the door. Max closed it quickly behind him. He went into the kitchen and took a glass, then returned to the living room and poured himself a healthy drink of whiskey. He didn't sit down, however; he had too much work to do.

When Max was finished inside, he headed out and sat on the hammock to wait for Lola. He thought about Lloyd. He imagined many times facing the man who shot him; however, the meeting they had just had was nothing like his imaginings. Once he saw Lloyd he realized that he didn't think of him as the man who had shot and nearly killed him; he thought of Lloyd as the man who had nearly shot Lola.

In the past, he had never worried about his work mixing with his personal life, because he had had no personal life, not really. Most of his life had been the work, the latest job. There had always been women, of course, but none that he would miss.

Now he realized that he had something—someone—precious. Someone he had won and never tired of—someone that he wanted to keep. For the first time in his life, Max realized that he had something to lose. The thought made him feel angry and frustrated and, worst of all, helpless.

He had seen something in Lloyd's eyes that last time in the SUV. He had seen the same thing today. Max had hurt him, his career, his pride, and Lloyd wanted to hurt him back. The only question was whether or not Lloyd realized how easy that would be now.

Perhaps a half hour later, a car from the tennis club stopped in front of the house to drop Lola off. Nick wasn't driving. *Smart boy,* Max thought. Lola walked toward him and Max felt an unreasonable sense of relief at seeing that she was all right.

"How was the rest of the lesson?" he asked.

"Not so good. His confidence was shattered," Lola said, heading past him and for the door.

"Don't go in there," he said.

"Why?" she asked, immediately on guard.

Then Max said two words he'd never said in their entire time together, words that he'd never used with a woman. "Let's talk."

"Okay, you've got me nervous. And I don't get nervous," she said.

"Agent Lloyd just left," Max said.

"What's he doing here?" she asked.

Max held up the brochure and handed it to her. "He came to show me this," he said as she looked over the paper with a professional eye. He watched her temper bubble up and show on her face. And then he realized that she wasn't angry at Agent Lloyd.

"Dammit, Max, is this what we're here for? Is it?" she asked.

"Babe, you chose this island. Remember?" he said.

"This isn't retirement at all. This is the next set-up, isn't it," she said, making it a statement, not a question. No, not a statement, an accusation.

"No, it's not," he said.

Lola looked hard into his eyes and said, "Don't think this is a gift from God. This is God toying with you."

Max wanted to protest that she was being unfair. He had never given a second's thought to stealing the diamond—not a second's *serious* thought, anyway. He wanted to tell her that she was wrong, that he was retired in his mind and in his heart and that he wanted nothing more than to live quietly with her.

He wanted to say all that but kept his tongue because he didn't want to lie and because he knew she would see right through the lie anyway. So Max kept his mouth shut and said nothing. Instead of talking, he got up and led her inside the house.

As soon as they opened the door, she could see that the place had been systematically dismantled. "Did Stan do this?" she asked.

"Sort of. I figured he bugged the place, so I started checking," he said.

Lola scanned the room. Max had overturned tables

57

and chairs and rolled up the rugs. He'd also taken apart the television, stereo, DVD player, and phone. "Did you find any?" she asked.

Max held up the tiny device in one hand. "Just the one he wanted me to find. There's another here somewhere."

Without hesitating, Lola started to look around. Max realized that he hadn't checked the bookshelf and started riffling through it, checking the spine of each book. Lola moved on to the thirty-five-millimeter camera, took the lens off and shook out the body. Nothing.

"Don't worry, I checked already. There's nothing in there," he said.

"That's the problem, there's nothing in here," she said. Was there another bug? Was Lloyd just toying with him, trying to make him doubt himself? Unfortunately, it seemed to be working.

Lola waved him toward the door.

They made their way to the beach and headed into the water, stopping when it was thigh-deep for Lola. When Max looked down at her, he saw that the anger was gone from her face. It was replaced by something he had never seen before in Lola: guilt.

"He took the fragment," she said, answering his unasked question.

"Fragment?" he asked.

"From the bullet he shot you with. I kept it to remind me of what I almost lost. Now it's gone," she said.

It was a mistake, no doubt about it. Unprofessional . . . and very touching. It was also of great concern. "That fragment puts me on the scene," Max said.

"I'll get it back," Lola said, with absolute confidence

in her voice, as if taking evidence from an obsessed FBI agent with a vendetta against them was as simple as going to the market. Looking at the set in her face, Max didn't doubt her for a second.

The Atlantis hotel was the most luxurious hotel on Paradise Island. Hell, it was probably the best hotel in all the Bahamas. And Stan had the smallest, crappiest room in the place. Well, no FBI expense account or salary would pay for a better room. In fact, Stan was lucky to be able to stay at this hotel at all.

Stan woke with a start, suddenly alert. Another knock and he was on his feet shuffling toward the door. A hotel concierge was there, greeting him with a wide smile. "Good morning, Mr. Lloyd. Your suite is ready," the young man said.

That woke him up. "Suite?" he asked.

The young man gave him a smug smile of condescension that Stan thought must have been invented by the employees of five-star hotels. "It's a bigger room," the concierge said.

Well, two could play at that game. "Why has it taken so damn long?" Stan said. The young man looked confused, at a loss for words for a moment. Stan thought the look suited him. "It was supposed to be ready when I checked in."

"I'm . . . sorry for the delay," the concierge said. "I will be happy to have the staff move your things there immediately. And I will be glad to show you the room myself."

"Fine," Stan said. "I'll be right with you."

Then Stan closed the door on the concierge and left him standing in the hallway. For a moment, Stan considering taking his time and maybe having a shower. He liked the idea of keeping the concierge waiting, but he had already had enough fun with the young man. And he had more pressing things on his mind . . . like what the hell was going on and who had arranged for him to have a suite?

Stan threw on his clothes and his gun. By the time he came out, there were two hotel bellhops waiting with a cart. "Careful with everything," he said, gesturing to his two ratty suitcases and the cases of equipment placed near them.

"Of course, sir," the concierge said. "This way," he added, leading Stan to an elevator.

A few seconds later, the elevator opened directly into a large room. At first Stan thought he was in a lobby, but he was actually in his new room, or one of them.

"Welcome to the world-famous Bridge Suite," the concierge said, a tinge of smugness in his voice again. Well, looking around, Stan understood. The room was nothing short of amazing—a glass penthouse, huge and luxurious. A big fancy breakfast was waiting for him on the table.

After a moment of gawking at the room, he realized that the concierge was speaking. "Breakfast is on the house," he said, passing Stan a handful of coupons. "And these are vouchers for free tennis lessons, complimentary skin exfoliant, seaweed body wrap, and facial scrub in the spa on the club level. Shirt and shoes are required in all public areas." The young man added a tinge of condescension for that last part, but Stan barely noticed, his mind whirring.

"That will be all," he said to the concierge. The bell-hops arrived with his things on a cart and he said, "Just leave it all on the bed."

When they were gone, Stan was tempted to forget everything else and dig in to the breakfast waiting for him. Well, he wasn't going to play that game. Not yet, at any rate. Instead, he dialed the phone. A moment later, he heard Burdett's voice say, "State your business." Burdett sounded busy, distracted. Good, that meant part of Stan's job was already done.

"You can't bribe me with a seaweed body wrap, Max. This doesn't buy you one bit of space. I'm going to be on you wherever you go," Stan said.

"It's no bribe, Stanley. I want you to see that if you lead the kind of life I do, stealing is the last thing on your mind," Burdett said. He sounded completely sin-cere and Stan didn't believe him for a second.

Stan looked down at the food. Accepting this room and eating that meal would violate about a dozen differ-ent Bureau regulations and a few laws as well. Then, be-fore he was even finished with that thought, two women arrived, holding a folding table. They were young, at-tractive, and very shapely.

"Mr. Lloyd?" the first woman said.

"Are you ready for your massage?" the second asked.

For a moment, Stan could only look at them, speech-less. "You son of a bitch," he said.

"I do the back," the first girl said.

"I do the front," the other replied.

Hell with it, Stan thought. He hadn't come here to play by the rules. He turned to the girls and smiled.

M ax was satisfied that they had checked the bedroom thoroughly enough. There wasn't a place or object that they hadn't checked that was still large enough to hold a bug. "Then our only choice is to ignore them both. Stan's just hoping to stir things up, trying to get to us," he said.

"Right. We can't let a low-rent government lackey interrupt our lives," Lola said. Then she smiled. It was an invitation and Max didn't need another one. He leaned down and kissed her.

The phone rang and the answering machine picked up almost immediately. "You've reached Max and Lola, we're at the beach, leave a message."

Putting a hand on the small of Lola's back, Max slowly started to move her toward the bed.

"Hey, guys, it's me," Lloyd's voice said from the phone. Immediately, Max froze as Lola did the same. They disengaged and stepped apart. "I hope I'm not interrupting, I'm just looking for tips on the local hot spots. Gimme a call when you have a chance . . ."

So Lloyd was just harassing them. Max found himself relax a degree. Then Lloyd added, "And Lola, 'low-rent government lackey'? That really stings."

Max froze and pulled away from Lola again. He could hear the smirk in Lloyd's voice. *Damn,* Max thought.

Where the hell is that thing? He scanned the room and realized he hadn't a clue even where to look. "Let's go out," Max said.

"Yeah," Lola replied.

As they headed out of the house, Max tried to relax. After all, Lloyd was only trying to rattle them. *And succeeding brilliantly,* he realized. Well, one small round would go to Lloyd, but this game was far from over.

Later at the restaurant, Max and Lola sat outside, overlooking the dance floor, where a Caribbean band played. The music was hypnotic and the night air smelled wonderful. By the end of the meal, Max felt like himself again.

An attractive woman approached the table. Max recognized her. She was a masseuse Lola used at the hotel. She smiled at Lola and dropped a small object into her hand.

"He hid it in a black jewelry box," she said.

"Good job," Lola said, smiling.

"Thank you," Max said to the girl who nodded and walked away.

Lola held up the bullet fragment. She kissed it once, then handed it to Max. "*You* get rid of it this time," she said.

"I will," Max replied.

"Good. Maybe I'll get lucky tonight. You know, we haven't made love since Stan's been here."

Max nodded. He'd realized the same thing. It was the

longest they'd gone since he'd recovered from his wound. "It's not us, it's him. You could bottle his personality and call it birth control."

"Maybe it *is* us. People have trouble adjusting to retirement. I really think you should *try* diving," Lola said.

A waiter appeared in front of them. Max saw first an extended napkin and then Lloyd looking down at him. Max kept his surprise from registering on his face. He'd be damned if he let the agent know that he was getting to him. "May I take your order?" Lloyd asked, pleasure in his voice.

Lola scowled and said, "No. I just lost my appetite."

"Just as well. I don't take orders from criminals. I arrest them," Lloyd said.

"Or fall asleep trying," Lola replied.

That stung, Max could see, but Lloyd covered it quickly. "So, you're admitting you were there?"

Shrugging, Lola said, "I read about it in the paper, like everyone else. You're famous."

Lloyd pulled over a chair and sat in it backward, his chest pushing against the chair's back. *That* nearly gave Max a start. It was a casual gesture that probably meant nothing, but Max knew it was also a classic wiseguy move. People who made their living with guns use little tricks like that all the time. The back of a chair would give limited protection from a bullet; it would also partially conceal hand movements.

Until the last job, Max had considered Lloyd a more or less capable FBI agent, but no match for him. Then Lloyd had surprised Max with a bullet in the shoulder.

Now this. Max wondered if Lloyd had any more surprises in him.

Shaking his head, Lloyd said, "I'm a *punch line*. But not for long. He who laughs last laughs loudest."

Across the room, Max saw two burly men guarding a door to a private dining room. A serious, young, dark-skinned woman approached them and flashed something at them. Max realized two things at once: first, she was local law enforcement, and, second, her expression wasn't just *serious*, it was *fierce*.

He forced his attention back on Lloyd and said, "By the way, return the movie, would you? The store called."

"I haven't finished it yet," Lloyd said.

"They catch the thief. But it's not who you think it is," Max said.

Shaking his head, Lloyd said, "I don't like those twist endings."

"Well, we don't like you," Lola said.

Max saw something was going on near the private dining room and said, "Lola, they're playing your song. Stan's lonely. Why don't you two dance?"

Lola, who no doubt had noticed the same thing Max had, took the hint immediately. "I'm feeling charitable, Stan," she said, making it clear from her tone that this was a peace offering.

"Really?" Stan said, genuinely surprised.

Lola led him away toward the dance floor. Max immediately shifted his eyes to the private dining room where the young woman, clearly a local constable, was looking past the two burly bodyguards inside the room.

From the open door, Max could see two local figures that he definitely recognized. The first was Henry Moore, a local crime lord with a large reputation on the island. He was in his indeterminate forties, lanky, with dark skin—Max assumed he was a local. Next to him was a white man with dark hair salted by grey. His name was Jean-Paul, who Max knew was a trusted associate of Moore's. Though Max had never met him, he assumed from the man's name Jean-Paul was French. Arranged around Jean-Paul was a small group of very beautiful women.

Moore kept his eyes on the constable waiting at the door as he said something to Jean-Paul. Max was impressed by the young policewoman. She was on the receiving end of a withering stare by a feared gangster and seemed completely unperturbed. Jean-Paul nodded and made his way out of the private room to the door where she was waiting.

"Get out of my way. Now," she said, standing her ground and speaking loud enough for Max to hear her from his table.

Jean-Paul refused to move and replied, "Monsieur Moore is currently socializing. Interrupting a man's leisure is harassment." There it was, the French accent.

"That's not harassment . . ." she said coolly. Then she reached out quickly with one hand and grabbed Jean-Paul in the crotch. One look at Jean-Paul's face told Max that she had a nice, tight grip on his balls. "Feel that? That's harassment."

The constable twisted her grip and Jean-Paul grunted

in pain. Whoever she was, she was tough. "Tell your boss this is only the beginning. I have two hands, and I can't be bought."

She let go of Jean-Paul's balls, turned, and walked off. Max got his first good look at her. She also had the dark skin of a local, and was very beautiful underneath that scowl she was wearing now.

Jean-Paul took a deep breath of relief, though Max could see that he was still in pain. Apparently, Max realized, there was a new sheriff in town. He hoped he never came up against her professionally.

As she headed for the door, Max stood up and said, "Excuse me, Constable."

The dance floor was crowded, and Lola found herself surrounded by hot, sweating bodies. For a few seconds she considered trying to keep an eye on the action near the private dining room but decided against it. She didn't want to make Lloyd suspicious. So she concentrated on Lloyd, knowing that Max would fill her in later. Lloyd wasn't much of a dance partner, but he make up for his lack of skill with enthusiasm.

Smiling, she said, "Listen, Stan. I know what you're doing. If you drag Max into your game, he will not lose."

"Eventually, they all lose," Lloyd said.

Lola shook her head. "Not my Max. He will make you look bad again. You should leave us alone. We're just a couple of retirees trying to enjoy the island life."

"All the same, I'll stick around, see what develops,"

Stan replied. The tempo of the music increased and Lloyd moved close, got more aggressive in his dancing. *More aggressive maybe,* she realized, *but with no more style than before.*

A woman approached. Lola turned and realized it was the woman who Max was watching spar with the thugs outside the private dining room.

"Excuse me . . ." she said, and Lola realized right away that she was some kind of cop. It was written all over her stance and body language.

Lloyd wasn't as observant. "In a second, honey. You'll get the chance," he said, his voice betraying both his cockiness and his cluelessness.

The woman flashed a badge and said, with complete confidence, "Police. Step off the dance floor." As the policewoman guided Lloyd off the floor, Lola found Max and they headed up the stairs.

Lola watched Lloyd try to follow them, but the woman drew her gun and pointed it at Lloyd. "Take another step, it'll be your last. Raise your hands, sir. Now."

"I'm law. Federal BI," Lloyd said, the cockiness gone from his voice, replaced by frustration. The policewoman pushed him toward a wall. Lloyd glanced back, as if noticing her for the first time. Lola understood. Flawless dark skin, long hair, high cheekbones, and a good figure: the woman was beautiful.

Glancing at Max, she saw that he was watching closely, an amused look on his face. Lloyd was trying to wriggle away, but in a flash the woman twisted his arm, pushing him into the wall roughly. A moment later, she pulled a gun from his shoulder holster.

"It's illegal to carry a concealed weapon on this island without a permit," she said.

"Hey, I'm working a suspect," Lloyd protested.

Continuing to twist his arm, the policewoman fished around in his coat pocket and said, "You're supposed to inform local authorities when you arrive . . . Agent Stanley P. Lloyd?"

Satisfied, Lola waved to Lloyd from the balcony of the restaurant as Max did the same. Then they headed for the exit, feeling better already. So Lloyd had been operating without any local sanction—as well as no jurisdiction. That meant what he had been doing was no more than harassing them. Lola felt a well of anger rise up. Lloyd had invaded their home, looked through their private things, and listened to them talk through the bug they still couldn't find.

And he had shot Max back in that warehouse.

Lola didn't think she could ever forgive Lloyd for that. She had seen the look in the agent's eyes when he had fired the gun and had almost taken from her the only part of her life that mattered. Lloyd had wanted to kill Max and had nearly succeeded.

Getting him into hot water with local cops was the least of what she wanted to do to Agent Lloyd, but it would have to do for a start.

Lloyd cursed Max as the woman behind him gave his arm another twist. Max had guessed Lloyd hadn't informed the local police he was there on a case. For once, Lloyd thought he was a step ahead of that arrogant bastard. Well, the game was far from over and Lloyd was far from finished with Max.

Let Max enjoy his childish revenge. Max had cost Lloyd plenty and he was determined to make Max pay with interest.

"Wait, you know him?" the woman behind him said.

"He's my suspect," Lloyd replied.

Reaching into his belt, she pulled out his gun. "We're still going to have to take this to the station and register it."

"That's ridiculous . . ." Lloyd said, but he knew he was getting off easy.

"Our laws are ridiculous? Your dancing, that was ridiculous," she said. She released his arm and pushed him toward the exit. "This way, Agent Lloyd. Welcome to paradise."

Chapter Five

This was the Bahamas. Paradise on earth. The island was even named Paradise. Nevertheless, Agent Lloyd thought that the police station he was sitting in at the moment looked depressingly like the ones he had seen across the United States: industrial, drab, utilitarian. His father and grandfather had worked in similar stations, and Lloyd had sworn that his life would be different.

So he went for the FBI. The offices were better, and the pay was better, and Lloyd had even seen a better class of felon. For years he was a rising star, using his natural aggressiveness and the street smarts he'd learned growing up in a traditional cop family as battering rams to close cases and make his mark on the FBI. He closed case after case and made some big arrests. He was pegged for assistant director early and might well have become one of the youngest in Bureau history. He was shaking up the buttoned-down FBI bureaucracy and making a name for himself.

And then he had gotten the assignment to run security for a new gem exhibit at the Smithsonian . . .

Stan checked the exhibit room himself, walking each square foot of the floor. The cameras were in place, both infrared and video. The motion sensors were up and running, and the live security guards were in place. Still, he checked each display case himself. The gems had just been put into place by the museum director and his staff, and Stan had breathed a sigh of relief when that was done. Security was always trickier for materials in transport than it was for things that stayed in one place.

This job was considered easy duty. The Smithsonian had its own security experts and always did a good job when opening a new exhibit. He was there to supervise and put the Bureau stamp on the whole thing. But he had done much more than that, personally overseeing security equipment, staffing, and procedures.

The museum director, a thin, nervous man named Robinson, hovered nervously over the displays. He always came back to the case that held the Napoleon necklace. It was the most valuable piece in the exhibit, with more than two dozen stones and total of two hundred and seventy-five carats. It was worth millions, and Stan had to admit it was beautiful, though he couldn't imagine where anyone would wear it. It would have been too much even on the red carpet at the Academy Awards.

"It'll be fine. I have everything under control," Stan said to the museum director.

Robinson turned to him and said, "It had better be. Do you know what it took to put this exhibit together? Years of work. And most of these pieces will be traveling when this is done, so if something goes wrong, it'll be ten more years before we see anything like it again."

Stan had gotten a genuine education on museum work. He knew that gems, or pieces of art, or whatever, often had their schedules set years in advance. Most of the work of a major exhibit was in the logistics and planning required in getting a large number of them into one place at one time.

It seemed like a silly occupation for an adult, but Robinson certainly took it seriously. He was apparently one of the best in the world at what he did; he was also very high-strung.

"Well, the security is one thing you don't have to worry about," Stan said to the man.

As he turned, Max noticed that the display case next to the Napoleon necklace was still empty. He had asked about it before and hadn't gotten a clear answer. "Mr. Robinson, are you still one short?" he asked, pointing to the empty display.

For a moment, Stan would have sworn that the director looked nervous—or even more nervous than usual.

"We're still waiting on a late delivery," Robinson said simply.

"How late? You open tomorrow," he said. There it was, a flash in the eyes, a twitch in the shoulders. If Stan didn't know better, he would have sworn that Robinson was hiding something.

"We can open without it if we have to," Robinson said.

"It's your show," Stan said and headed out to visit the control room. The Smithsonian Institution had among the best and most cutting-edge security systems in the world. Good security was necessary since almost all of the objects on display in the acres of public and storage areas were one-of-a-kind and many of them priceless. Nevertheless, Stan had made sure that the security system here was top-notch. In addition to state-of-the-art technology, Stan had also insisted on having plenty of live guards on-site for the first month.

For a number of reasons, theft was more likely in the first weeks or days of a major exhibit. Part of it was the psychology of the new challenge that some thieves found too tempting to resist. And part of it was the fact that a traveling exhibit would often only stay in one place for a short period. Even if the pieces were part of the Smithsonian's permanent collection, exhibits were cycled in and out regularly.

The public areas of the Smithsonian were incredibly large and spread out over a number of museums, including one as far away from Washington as New York. The Smithsonian's Arts and Industries building was a large old brick structure. Nicknamed "the Castle," it was beautiful, with two towers in the front and thousands of square feet of display space, with even more space for storage.

He knew the building was one of the first built as part of the Smithsonian and opened in 1881. The very age of the place was of some concern to Stan. He would have much preferred a newer building made with modern security considerations in mind. The fact was, though the building looked good on the outside, it was badly in need of upgrades. Still, he had done a good job for security for the gem exhibit and had confidence in his system.

Before Stan reached the control room, he saw Field Office Chief Kirsh in the hallway. "Checking up on me, Chief?" Stan asked good-naturedly.

"You bet," Kirsh replied. Stan understood. Despite the high stakes, security for a museum exhibit was not a sexy assignment and, normally, no one in the Bureau hierarchy would pay much attention—unless something went wrong.

In this case, Director Robinson was connected to someone high up in the Bureau. And some of the gems were on loan from foreign governments. A loss would be pretty embarrassing. Well, Stan had planned carefully and would not be surprised.

"How's Robinson?" Chief Kirsh asked.

"He's about to have a stroke," Stan said.

"No change, then?" Kirsh said, smiling.

"We'll be fine, Chief," Stan said. "I can stay the night to keep an eye on things, and then the first few hours after they open the exhibit in the morning."

"I appreciate that, Stan. And I appreciate you taking this assignment. I know it's not exactly a career-making case, but people are watching. This will be good for you," Kirsh said.

Stan had made no bones about his ambition in the Bureau. He hoped to be field office chief in a year or two, and then, if he did well there, he wanted to be the youngest assistant director in the Bureau's history. A few visible assignments and a few big cases and he might just do it. With plans like that, staying up all night on a few extra cups of coffee was the least he could do.

"You can count on me, Chief," Stan said.

The chief put a hand on Stan's shoulder and said, "I have no doubt that's true, son."

Chief Kirsh was a fair enough boss. He had languished in a field office out west for years before getting transferred to the D.C. office, which also happened to be in the FBI headquarters building. With such close proximity to headquarters, it was well known that a D.C. field office assignment was a fast track for ambitious agents. Agents working there weren't supposed to have any advantage over agents in other field offices, but like many things in the Bureau, the reality was very different from the ideal.

Though an Ivy League graduate himself, Kirsh didn't have any of the snobbish attitude that some of the agents had toward Stan's New Jersey state college education. For many agents in the Bureau, better to be bottom of the class at Brown than top of the class at a good state school like Rutgers University.

Well, Stan had a saying for those agents: Fuck 'em.

He'd put himself through college and then graduated near the top of his class at Quantico. They'd be eating his dust soon enough and be saluting him when he made assistant director.

"I'll go see if I can calm Mr. Robinson down," Kirsh said. Stan nodded to him and stepped into the control room. The monitors were on and he had two of the best Smithsonian security men, both ex-military, watching them and the security board.

"How's it look, boys?" Stan asked.

"Good, sir," the guards replied in chorus. Just then, a red light lit up on the board and flickered for a moment before going out again.

"What the—" Stan began.

"Nothing, sir, we've been getting intermittent flags on one of the storage area sensors," the guard said.

"Have you been checking it out?" Stan asked.

"Each time. It's probably just a bad sensor," the guard replied.

"Well, check it out again and get someone from maintenance to look at it," Stan said.

"Will do," the guard said.

Stan wasn't overly concerned. All of the valuable gems had already been moved from the storage area. Still, he wanted to make sure his report was spotless. If people were watching him from on high, he wouldn't give them anything to complain about.

Stan watched the monitors and security board himself for a few minutes over the shoulders of the guards. It was quiet, and Stan was sure it would be for the rest of the night. His biggest problem would likely be dealing with the boredom and keeping awake. That reminded him that it was time for coffee, and he headed for the door.

"Coffee run—you boys want some?" Stan asked.

They both said yes, and as Stan left, one of them said, "Maintenance has arrived at the storage area."

"Good," Stan said. This would be a real tight operation. And the report might not be sexy, but it would be so clean you could eat off of it. He headed for the employee break room, where the coffee machine sat. Planning ahead, he'd brought plenty of singles for the machine and began feeding it.

A few minutes later, he was carrying three cups of coffee back to the control room when the alarm sounded. His first thought was that it had to be a mistake. His second thought was that if it wasn't, he was pretty well screwed.

Then it registered that this was the loud Klaxon of a general alarm, which, under the circumstances, could only mean a theft in progress. Stan didn't wait another second; he dropped the coffee on the hallway floor and ran like hell for the exhibit room, drawing his gun as he moved.

He was there in less than half a minute and saw that Kirsh looked stricken, while museum director Robinson looked like he was about to explode. Stan rushed into the room, scanning for the perp as he led with his gun.

"Where is he, Chief?" Stan said.

Kirsh didn't respond right away. In fact, he didn't respond at all, but one thing was clear. No one was here. Reaching for his radio, Stan pulled it from his belt and said, "Talk to me."

The control room guard said, "We have a problem at the storage area."

"I know, a bad sensor. Who the hell hit the general alarm for that?" Stan barked.

"No, it's not just a sensor. We're showing an open door and we have an agent down. Friedman is unconscious," the guard said.

"What?" Stan exclaimed. He turned to see Director Robinson on his knees on the floor, his hands on his head. To the chief, he said, "There's nothing in the storage room."

Something strange crossed the chief's face as Robinson moaned. There was something very odd going on here. It didn't take a genius to figure out that the chief and the director knew something they weren't telling him. Whatever it was, it involved the storeroom and something valuable.

"Chief?" Stan said.

"Agent Lloyd, there was one piece that we kept in storage. We didn't . . ."

Stan didn't wait to hear the explanation. He didn't have time and he was pretty sure it would just piss him off. He raced into the corridor and headed for the exit, hauling ass. If a thief had made off with something from the storeroom, there was only one way out of the complex. And if the thief hadn't made it to Jefferson Drive yet, there was still a chance.

Racing past the guards at the door, Stan headed outside. He didn't bother to head around to the storage area. Anyone ballsy enough to try something with federal agents all around would not stay put. And if the thief was still on the grounds, Stan knew he would have only seconds to catch him.

In the open air, Stan scanned the night for any vehicles on the one-lane paths that were the only way out. There was only one, a maintenance van that Stan dismissed.

Wait, a voice inside said. Stan remembered that a few minutes before the alarm, a maintenance man had arrived to check the sensor. Suddenly, everything made sense and Stan took off at a full run. The paths winded through the grounds, and Stan had one chance to cut him off on foot. He headed across the grass toward the point where the path connected to the parking lot, which then emptied onto Jefferson Drive. It would be close, very close, but he knew he had a shot.

Stan was less than a hundred yards from the exit when he saw the van speed up through the parking lot. Stan knew he'd been had. The thief was now dropping all pretense and getting the hell out of Dodge. Drawing his gun, Stan saw the van take the turn out of the lot and onto Jefferson.

He was still fifty yards away, but he didn't hesitate. Stan fired as he ran, aiming high at the back of the van. Then he fired again, and again, trying to empty the entire clip of his nine-millimeter into the van as it sped away. Once it hit the open road, the van sped up even more and put still more distance between them. After his last shot, Stan saw one of the rear windows of the van shatter before it was out of range—which was just as well because he was out of bullets.

Son of a bitch, Stan thought as he watched the taillights disappear on Jefferson Avenue and into the night.

He walked back to the building, as confused as he was pissed. What the hell had been taken if the exhibit items were safe? Chief Kirsh was waiting for him at the door. "Chief, what the hell is going on here?" he asked.

"I'll handle this, Agent Lloyd," the chief said.

"But sir, I don't even know—"

"You're off duty until tomorrow. Go home, get some sleep," Kirsh said.

Stan did go home, but he didn't get much sleep. He was at Kirsh's office at nine and had to wait for a few minutes before Kirsh saw him. When he finally entered the room, Stan didn't waste any time. "What happened last night, sir?"

To his surprise, Kirsh looked nervous. He didn't speak right away. Instead, he seemed to be sizing Stan up, then finally said, "Agent Lloyd . . ." So it was *Agent Lloyd* now, not Stan. Kirsh hesitated for a moment and said, "There was a theft last night at the museum, a very valuable piece was lost. Agent Johnson was drugged— chloroform we think—but he's doing fine now."

"Sir, that's impossible. I was there—every major piece was accounted for," Stan said.

"Not every piece . . . there was another," Kirsh said.

"Chief, there's obviously something I don't know here. Please bring me into the loop," Stan said. He had a very bad feeling about the way this was going.

"The piece was called the Napoleon diamond. It was one of three, more than fifty carats and worth in the tens of millions," Kirsh said, his voice tight.

"The Napoleon diamond? We had a Napoleon neck-lace . . ." Stan said.

"The diamond was a single stone, very valuable and on loan from the French government," Kirsh said.

Stan was starting to get angry. This didn't make any sense and he had a sick feeling that this was going to end very badly for him. "Sir, I was running security for the exhibit. How could it be that I didn't know about the most valuable piece?"

"The museum director and the Bureau had special security in place for this diamond," Kirsh said.

"Special security?" Stan asked.

"A decision was made at very high levels to keep the diamond's part in the exhibit a secret until opening. The museum director wanted to make a dramatic unveiling and we thought secrecy was the best possible security," Kirsh said.

"Apparently, it was not the *best possible security*," Stan said.

"Clearly," Kirsh said, his voice tight. Stan saw that his chief was having trouble looking him in the eye. There was another level to this, but he'd be damned if he could figure it out.

"Sir, this is completely unacceptable. I was the agent in charge and was denied vital information. If I'd known about the diamond I could have taken additional precautions. Hell, I didn't know about it and I still almost got the bastard," Stan said.

"I know. Good work there, Agent Lloyd. That certainly speaks well for you and will help you come out of this one okay," Kirsh said.

"With all due respect, sir, I don't need any help. I've done nothing wrong, and my report will show—"

Kirsh silenced him with a hand and stood up. "This is a very delicate matter. I will write the report," he said.

"Sir?" Stan said, the sick feeling in his stomach getting worse.

Coming around the desk to face him, Kirsh said, "Stan . . ." There it was, he was *Stan* again. "No one wants you to take all the blame for this one."

"*All* the blame? I don't deserve *any* of it," Stan said.

Leaning back on his desk, Kirsh said, "Stan, you know that you're part of a team. You're a good agent, maybe a great one. You've broken some big cases, made some important arrests. And at every turn, you've had my support and the support of your fellow agents. You've had the support of the rest of *the team*. As a result, you've come very far very fast, especially for someone with your background and education."

What he was really saying was, *You've come very far for the son of a Jersey City cop, for someone who went to a state college.*

That was the kind of condescending bullshit he'd had to put up with from the agents and higher-ups from Brown, Yale, and Harvard who thought they owned the fast track and held the keys to the executive crapper.

When he spoke, he had to work to keep his voice even. "Sir, I haven't let the team down," he said.

"No, you did good work last night and it all went to hell anyway. And like I said, you won't take all the blame," Kirsh said.

"But I don't deserve *any* of the blame," Stan repeated, nearly shouting it this time. He was suddenly sure of who was behind the particular screw up. No wonder Kirsh was on-site last night. It must have been his brilliant idea to keep the diamond a secret. The only problem was that somebody leaked that little detail to the crooks and nobody told the guy in charge of security.

"Now hold on. Watch your tone with me, Agent. You don't want to be written up for insubordination after what happened last night," Kirsh said.

There was the threat, Stan realized. *Go along or pay a price*. Stan held his tongue. It was the hardest thing he'd done in weeks—hell, months.

Kirsh smiled and said, "My report will show that after the . . . incident, your actions were exemplary. That will mitigate things somewhat. Stan, you're young—you'll recover from this. And even if you're in the doghouse for a little while, you and I know that you're taking one for the team. I won't forget this." Then Kirsh looked him straight in the eye and said, "Do we understand each other?"

Stan remembered his feeling last night when things started to go to hell. He was right then: he was pretty well screwed. "Perfectly," he said in the end.

"Come back after lunch. I'll need you to sign the report," Kirsh said.

After lunch, Stan had signed the report. A bigger pile of bullshit he had never seen before. But Kirsh had made good on his promise. Stan didn't take *all* the blame; he had shared it with the Smithsonian security guards and the hapless agent Johnson who'd gotten chloroform in the face. As it turned out, Kirsh had taken none of the blame, though he did take *decisive action* after the fact and had put a written reprimand in

Stan's file. The reprimand had cited *significant errors in judgment*.

No, not *pretty* well screwed, *very* well screwed.

After that, Lloyd had tried his damnedest to recover the diamond with no luck. In the next few years, he had made some big cases and had largely rehabilitated his stalled career. And then there had been another security assignment and another theft and Stan had been set back again.

This time he had a suspect, though: Max Burdett, a man who already had a file at the Bureau connecting him to other important heists. However, Burdett had an alibi—a good one—and Stan hadn't been able to prove anything. Yet the more he looked into Burdett, the more sure he had become. Max had been the one behind the robbery as well as the theft of the first Napoleon diamond.

And then the assignment came to run security for the second Napoleon diamond and Stan saw his chance. He had lobbied hard for the assignment and got it. Now he finally had a chance to redeem himself and get his career back on track. So he had set up what he thought was airtight security at the Staples Center. As he made his preparations, Stan knew he would not be the youngest assistant directory in Bureau history, but he had still been confident that he would get there.

That was, of course, before Burdett had made him a laughingstock at the Bureau and in the press, which ran endless stories about the theft.

FEDERAL AGENT FALLS ASLEEP ON THE JOB AS THIEF MAKES OFF WITH LOOT.

Stan hadn't found any of the headlines funny, but there sure had been a lot of them. And Stan had gotten a new nickname around the office: Sleeping Beauty.

Chapter Six

Officer Sophie St. Vincent interrupted Stan's reverie by clearing her throat. Then she held up his ID and said, "The watermarks and holograms match. Your ID's good. Where's your partner? You guys usually work in pairs," she said.

"He's on the case stateside," Stan said, answering more quickly than he would have liked. Sophie accepted it, however, and merely said, "I still have to register the gun," keeping her face neutral. He realized that he hadn't seen anything but a scowl or a frown on her face since he'd met her at the restaurant.

Now she was frowning into the paperwork on her desk

as she filled out forms, presumably to register his gun.

"You have a nice smile," he said.

"I haven't smiled at you," she said seriously.

"You will," he said, giving her a smile of his own.

She didn't return the smile, but Stan wasn't troubled. He liked a challenge.

Before he could make his next move, a large, handsome man wearing the uniform of the police captain entered. He was dark-skinned, another local, with a large mustache. Lloyd had made it a point to learn his name. It was Captain Zacharias Bethel.

"Officer Sophie St. Vincent, what a pleasant surprise," he said. Whatever was going on, he was annoyed at Sophie. She bristled immediately. "I'm getting complaints about you bothering Henry Moore."

"Just doing my job," Sophie replied, keeping her tone even—which took some effort for her, Lloyd noticed.

"The man's practically the unofficial mayor of the island. In one year he's made everyone here like him. Something you haven't been able to do in a lifetime," Captain Bethel said.

Then Lloyd could see that Sophie had lost whatever battle was raging inside her to keep her tongue. "I guess I'm not the kiss-ass politician that you are, Zacharias," she said coolly.

Instead of being furious, the captain seemed almost amused. There was something going on here, but Lloyd couldn't figure out what it was yet. "I want you to stay behind tonight so we can discuss your attitude," Captain Bethel said, putting his hand on her shoulder and giving it a suggestive squeeze.

That did it for Sophie. She handed Lloyd his gun and stood up. "You knew about my attitude the day we got married and the day we got divorced. You're not gonna learn any more about it tonight. Besides, I have plans. With Special Agent Lloyd of the FBI. He's just arrived on the island," she said.

This was a surprise to Stan. He had expected to have to work on Sophie for a few days at least before she went out with him. He would have enjoyed the chase. But now she was going to give him his chance just because she wanted to piss off her ex-husband. Well, these days Lloyd took his victories where he could find them.

"Is that so?" Captain Bethel asked him.

Her eyes were asking him to play along, but Stan had already made up his mind. "Yep," he said to the captain. Then he stood up and offered his arm to Sophie. "Shall we?" he asked.

"We shall," she replied, taking his arm.

They headed for the door. Before they left the station, Stan turned and gave the captain his most winning smile. Bethel's eyes burned and Stan was pleased with himself. He had expected to run the situation with Burdett under the radar of local law enforcement. Now he realized there might be additional benefits to interagency cooperation.

From their bedroom, Max looked out through the open shutters at the ocean. He heard Lola approaching, and then she was wrapping her arms around him from behind.

"Isn't it beautiful?" she asked.

"Yes," Max replied.

"Is it enough?" she asked. Once again, he was struck by how she was able to very nearly read his mind.

"Of course it is," was all he said. Turning to her, he kissed her in the moonlight, in their house overlooking the ocean. It would have been enough for anyone, should have been enough for him. Yet he found himself opening his eyes and looking out to the ocean where he could see a dazzling series of lights emerge from a huge and magnificent cruise ship, the *Seven Seas Navigator,* which coasted toward the port, sliding across the water.

Their kiss ended and Max realized that Lola was looking at the ship, too. "You know what Oscar Wilde said? The only way to get rid of temptation is to yield to it," he said.

"And he ended his life rotting away in a cold prison. I say, turn your back on temptation, or substitute something *more* tempting . . ." Lola said, kissing him. Then she reached out and snapped the shutters closed, blocking out the view. "See how easy that was?" she says.

Pushing him back onto the bed, Lola landed on top of him. Her sarong fell open and he saw that she was wearing new lingerie. Black La Perla lace lingerie, in fact—his favorite. As they kissed, Max found himself catching glimpses of the glittering ship through the mirror, which was pointed to the window. The *Seven Seas Navigator* was moving slowly but inexorably toward the port.

The diamond is moving slowly but inexorably toward the port, his mind added.

From the corner of his eye, he saw that Lola was watching it as well, no doubt thinking the same thing. The jig was up and both of them gave an embarrassed smile.

This has gone too far, Max thought. It was one thing to think about work; it was another thing to let work interfere in *this* part of their life. Max pulled on the nearby curtain and blocked the view.

"What would you like to see, Special Agent Lloyd?" Sophie asked. "There are quite a few beautiful restaurants, some nice clubs."

They hadn't spoken about what had happened back at the station. But clearly she was grateful for his help with her captain and ex-husband. And she was offering to show him around the island.

"Well, I am hungry," Lloyd said.

As they got into her car, she said, "Some of the hotel—"

"No hotels, no fancy restaurants, no tourist traps. Show me the real Paradise Island, show me *your* island," Lloyd said.

She nodded and Lloyd got the feeling that she was pleased. "Then leave everything to me," she said.

They ended up in front of a place called Goldie's Conch Shack. The name was accurate. It wasn't much more than a shack, full mostly of locals and a few others who looked like they belonged there.

In the center of the restaurant, there was a long bench where a cook used a small hatchet to crack open the base of a conch shell. Then he used a knife to impale the mollusk inside, laying it out on a board to be eaten by the customers around the bench.

As Sophie watched the process, Lloyd stole a look at her figure. She was attractive, very attractive. And he knew she was single . . .

She was also a good cop who missed nothing. She caught him looking at her and said, "I see what you're thinking, and you can forget it. Guys come down to the island looking for a slice of paradise with a local girl, and they'll say anything to get it."

Lloyd lifted up his hands to protest his innocence. "Hey, I was just—"

She waved off his speech and was all business. "How long have you been chasing Max?"

"Seven years. Since the first Napoleon diamond went missing. I got to the scene, took a few shots at the getaway car. The next day, a bottle of champagne arrived for me at FBI headquarters. The note said: 'Aim for the tires next time.'"

Sophie nodded. "He was baiting you."

"I couldn't put a name to him until a few years ago," Stan added, passing Sophie another conch.

"Is there a money trail?" she asked. Her eyes were alert, focused, and Lloyd had the feeling that they were showing him only a part of what was going on behind them. She was sharp, this one. Lloyd had been interested before. Now he was determined to get to know her better.

"Everything's clean: taxes, bank accounts. He doesn't buy expensive paintings, nothing. I think it's more about the challenge. And the alibi. That's his work of art."

Lloyd remembered Burdett's smug face on the screen at the Lakers game—while he was lifting the diamond. It had to be a tape, of course, but he must have had some serious inside help because the tape had never been recovered.

"It sounds like you admire him," Sophie said.

Stan shrugged. "Would I like to live one day in his velvety slippers? Maybe. But I don't admire him. He's beaten me too many times for that," Lloyd said.

"Maybe you need a female touch," she said.

"It's what I need alright." Stan replied.

"Listen: I want a big arrest. You need local help. I'll extend the FBI courtesy on this one, as long as I'm riding shotgun," she said coolly.

She was right, of course. Out here, in unfamiliar territory, he could use help. It wasn't the offer he'd been hoping for, but it was they best one he'd had all day—hell, the best in a long time.

The next morning, an odd noise woke Max from his sleep. He dressed and walked outside to see Lola wielding a skill-saw. There was a stack of pressure-treated lumber next to her as she cut one piece to size.

She saw him immediately and nodded. "What's going on?" he asked, raising his voice to make himself heard over the noise.

"I'm building a deck," she replied, nearly shouting.

"You're trying to stay busy," he said.

Turning off the saw, Lola said, "Sometimes a deck's

just a deck. But we're going to get married on this one. And we'll sit here and watch sunsets until we get old."

"Can't wait," Max said, immediately regretting his sarcasm. He turned to go.

"Where are you going?" she asked.

"You said I need a hobby. I guess I'll go find one," he said.

Two workers arrived carrying more lumber. They approached Lola, and one of them said, "Excuse me, ma'am. Where do you want the wood?"

Lola pointed to a spot near the wood framing and said, "Right there."

The worker pointed at a spot nearby and said, "Here?"

Without hesitating, Lola glanced back at the spot and picked up a screwdriver, hurling it straight into a two-by-six that was a full twenty feet away.

"Right there. Thank you," she said sweetly.

Max smiled at the workers' surprised expressions and headed for his car. By the time he started the Camaro he had a destination in mind. A few minutes later, he was at the marina. For his entire adult life, his work had been all-consuming. It hadn't left him much time for hobbies of any kind. Still, he had always had a deep appreciation for beautiful things. And he knew that he was standing in front of something very beautiful.

After parking the car, he stepped out and looked at the *Seven Seas Navigator*. It was very large—twenty stories tall and one thousand seventy-four feet in length. It had two full-size movie theaters, a grand ballroom, four swimming pools, three full gymnasiums, a planetarium, and room for thousands of passengers.

The ship was a marvel of both engineering and aesthetics. And it could accommodate passengers in either simple staterooms or three-thousand-square-foot luxury suites that rivaled the accommodations at the best hotels in the world. The ship was an amazing achievement, yet the most amazing thing about it at the moment was a piece of cargo that was not created by man. It weighed only a few ounces and had been formed deep in the earth by incredible forces over millions of years.

Passengers walked up and down the access ramps. Max decided that it wouldn't hurt to take a closer look at the ship. It wasn't a hobby, exactly, but as long as he didn't do anything, there was no harm in it.

Henry Moore watched the ship from the dock. He was prepared to wait all day, but, as it turned out, his wait was much shorter than he'd expected. One of the security guards on his payroll called in and said, "He's here."

Jean-Paul, who was holding an umbrella over Moore's head, nodded. Moore scanned the access ramps and finally found Max Burdett. Over the years in his many legal and illegal businesses Moore had become a student of human nature.

One of the many things that he had observed was that exceptional people behaved exceptionally. They did what they did because they could do no other. It was true of great athletes, artists, musicians, and a certain class of criminal—criminals like Max Burdett. He was a rare combination of raw talent, study, determination, and nerve.

What life was there for a star quarterback after his career was over? What life was there for Burdett in retirement? The answer to both questions was none.

Ballplayers would play well past the limits of reason and safety. Near the end of his career, Joe Namath had risked being crippled for life because his knees had been so badly injured time and time again. After his career finally ended Namath could still walk, miraculously enough, but he did so only with serious pain. Was it worth it? Men like that didn't even consider the question. They simply did what they were made to do for as long as they could.

The rumor was that Burdett had been shot on his last job. The next job might cost him his life, but Moore didn't think that would stop him. In fact, Henry Moore was counting on it . . .

Chapter Seven

Max walked along the sky deck of the ship. He passed the main pool where people were swimming and sunbathing. Nearby, there was a volleyball game in progress and someone was climbing a rock wall. The place was bustling with activity, which made it easier for Max to blend in.

He had to physically shake off that thought. That was the kind of thinking he used to do when he was at the beginning of a job. And this *wasn't a job*. He was retired and, as such, he was just showing a professional interest—a *casual* professional interest—in the gem exhibit on board the ship. According to the literature, it was world-class. The fact that it had one of the Napoleon diamonds alone made it worth a look.

Following signs, Max headed for the exhibit. As he passed the large ballroom, he saw a sign outside that read THEME PARTY SATURDAY NIGHT: KING NEPTUNE'S UNDERSEA BALL. Following signs, he found the gem exhibit, which was a large room with excellent quality stones throughout. Diamonds, rubies, sapphires . . . all of the precious stones were represented. And most of them were top-notch, in size and quality as well as cut. He had *acquired* better jewels than most of what was on display, but not many. He was also impressed by the displays themselves. The curator had showed a little bit of style, using lighting and arrangement to good effect.

A tour guide was leading a group of tourists around the exhibit room. She pointed to an adjoining room and said, "The centerpiece of our exhibit . . ." Sitting in an impregnable-looking octagonal room sat a large stand holding a glass display case.

And there it was: the third Napoleon diamond.

Max moved closer, his heart racing. He had to use his professional skills to keep excitement from showing on his face. Nearby was an impressive portrait of Napoleon holding his diamond-studded sword.

The guide continued as Max stepped closer. "Napoleon had three priceless diamonds set into the hilt of his sword. After his defeat, they were pried out and dispersed around the globe. This is one of the rare occasions the last remaining diamond is on public display . . ." Then the guide moved on, showing off another display. "And next we have some rare South African gems . . ."

Max tuned her out and stood in front of the diamond. After a few seconds, he realized that he had forgotten to breathe. Chiding himself, he took a casual breath and stared at the stone. It was magnificent. There were only three in the world. Max, of course, had acquired the first two. He'd traced this one's movements for years and had even come up with some preliminary plans to get it, but the others had presented more attractive targets at the time.

When he'd retired, he'd made a conscious decision to forget this one. Now fate had brought it nearly to his door. *It could be done,* a little voice in the back of his mind said. He didn't doubt that voice, though the security he had seen was very good. Max had no doubt that there were half a dozen security measures he had not seen that would make this one a challenge, if not impossible . . .

Still, impossible or not, Max had no doubt that it could be done, that *he* could do it. He and Lola.

There it was: the problem. He wouldn't work a big job without her, but he would never put her in danger again. For what? Another diamond like the ones he'd already taken? Another challenge? For a moment, he allowed himself to imagine the job, how it would feel, the anticipation, the rush of excitement during the job, the satisfaction at the end . . . and that inevitable letdown when it was all done and he realized that the getting was much better than the having.

Lola. The risk was too great. They already had more money than they needed. And even if he did pull off the job, what then? There were only three Napoleon diamonds, what would he do when he'd stolen them all?

Retire, his mind supplied. Well, he'd done that already, in style, with the one thing, the one person who had never disappointed him. Max had found Lola to be an exception to his rule: having her was just as good as winning her.

There were footsteps behind him, and before Max could turn around he heard Lloyd's voice say, "Cute little rock."

Agent Lloyd took up a place next to him as Max said, "You're like a bad penny—you keep turning up."

"No, I'm the gum on the bottom of your shoe. Where you go, I go."

Keeping his eyes fixed on the diamond, Max replied, "You're gonna be bored. I'm just here to look."

Max's peripheral vision told him that Lloyd was studying him. "Don't tell me you lost your peach pits back in that warehouse when you took Napoleon two," Lloyd said. When Max didn't respond, he continued, "Doesn't matter, with six cameras, four stationary, two revolving . . ."

Max had seen the cameras, their lenses almost completely hidden in the corners of the room. Of course, the real number was eight. Lloyd had obviously missed two, or was playing a game with him.

"A dozen IR sensors—" Lloyd continued.

Max didn't let that one go. "Sixteen. You missed the ones at ankle level," he said.

"Plus your standard twenty-four-hour rotating guards, hourly shifts . . ." Lloyd parried.

"Unbreakable four-inch glass display controlled by an uncopyable magnetic keycard . . ."

"I just realized: you could never get it anyway," Lloyd said.

Turning to face Lloyd, Max had to suppress his anger at the schoolyard-level taunt. It was insulting for Lloyd to think that it might be effective, and it was infuriating to Max that part of him was responding and silently protesting that he *could* get around all of the security measures. Some of them he had already figured out ways around, the others . . . his mind was working on those already and would continue to do so almost without conscious thought. To Lloyd, he simply said, "You're right. It's impossible."

Max turned and left Lloyd standing there in front of the diamond.

Quickly making his way through the ship, Max approached the exit ramp to head down to the marina.

"Nice move last night," a female voice said from behind him.

Max cursed himself. Twice in the last twenty minutes police had snuck up on him. He really was losing his edge. Perhaps it was best that he'd retired. Putting a smile on, he turned and said, "I wanted you to meet, Stan. You're both cops—I hoped you'd hit it off."

"Be careful what you wish for," she said, the warning clear in her voice.

The warning was serious and Max had figured out that this woman was not to be trifled with. She had walked up to Henry Moore himself and laid down a challenge in public. There was steel in her eyes and Max realized he would have to consider her carefully . . . if he was going to go after the diamond, which, of course, he was not.

Max could see Lloyd approaching. He nodded to Officer St. Vincent and continued on his way to the ramp.

Standing on the other side of the exit ramp, Lola watched Max approach and then cross. She kept herself hidden until he stepped off and headed for his car. She waited another few seconds until Lloyd and the policewoman lost interest in watching Max and moved along themselves.

Lola was on the ship a few seconds later and quickly found her way to the gem exhibit. In front of the last Napoleon diamond, Lola understood what was driving Max lately. It was amazing, easy to get lost in . . . and easy to lose your life over.

Automatically, Lola found herself inventorying the cameras, motion sensors, and other security measures. It would be very difficult, but nothing was impossible.

The tug was strong, she realized, even for her, and she had adapted to retirement much better than Max. Lola had loved her work, loving it even more when she and Max had started doing it together. But that work had almost cost her Max, and as much as she loved this sort of challenge, she loved Max more.

*　*　*

Less than a second before Max was to open the door of his car, he felt a hand on his back. "Get in. We're taking a ride," a male voice behind him said in a French accent. Max didn't recognize the voice immediately, but he recognized the tone. Whoever it was, this man was trouble—and Max was using great personal restraint these days to stay out of trouble.

"I don't think so," Max said.

There was movement next to him. Turning, Max saw who he was dealing with: it was Jean-Paul, the man he had seen at the restaurant who worked for Henry Moore. Max *was* right; he was trouble, and he was carrying a gun in the front of his pants.

"Maybe you want to think again," Jean-Paul said.

Max opened the door and felt himself being pushed inside. A moment later, Jean-Paul climbed into the passenger seat. Pulling out of the Marina, Max noted they were being followed by a nondescript sedan, Jean-Paul's backup, no doubt.

Following Jean-Paul's directions, Max drove deeper into the island. On some level, he had been aware that the beachfront life, the life of good restaurants and hotels, was a fantasy, a show for the tourists and wealthy residents. Well, if that part of the island was a show, this was the backstage.

Stores were run-down, dirty, and graffiti-smeared. Locals sat on curbs, eating fruit as chickens and mules roamed freely. This didn't just look like another island; it looked like another world. At Jean-Paul's direction, Max pulled up to a decaying three-story brick colonial building. Like everything around it, the structure had seen better days, though it still showed signs of those more prosperous times, including outdoor walkways on every level.

Inside, Jean-Paul guided Max through a series of corridors and stairways with doors on either side. Max had been upset with himself for letting Lloyd and Officer St. Vincent get the drop on him, but the stakes had been low there. Unless he committed a crime, they had nothing on him.

One of Henry Moore's gunmen paying him a visit was a rather large and unpleasant surprise. Agent Lloyd had said that he didn't like surprise endings. On that, Max had to agree with him. The fact was that in Max's line of work surprises were almost always bad and too often dangerous, if not fatal. Well, this one couldn't be helped. All he could do was what he'd do on a job: improvise.

"You're very fortunate. Not many people are given time with Mr. Moore," Jean-Paul said pleasantly.

"I feel lucky," Max replied.

"Be careful. Good manners are a priority with him," the gunman added.

At the end of the hallway, Max saw two large men, obviously bodyguards, standing in front of a door. They opened it, allowing Jean-Paul and Max to enter the room. It was a book-lined office. Sitting behind his large, oak, executive desk, wearing glasses and an impeccable suit and loafers, sat Henry Moore. The man stood, giving Max a warm smile. "A pleasure to meet you, Mr. Burdett," Moore said in American-accented English.

"You're American? Henry Moore?" Max asked.

"My name's Henry Moore. I placed the thing on the 'e.' Moore. It's more appropriate to my surroundings," he said, flashing Max a charming smile. "I imagine you're wondering why you're here. To put it bluntly, the impoverished people of this island need your help."

Moore had spoken with complete seriousness, his tone earnest. This was another surprise, and Max was immediately suspicious. Glancing around the office, he saw framed photos of Nelson Mandela, Che Guevara, Fidel Castro, The Mamas & The Papas—all of them populist icons.

Of course, Max knew a thing or two about Che and Castro. Both had been revolutionaries "for the people" but were also brutal men with more than their share of blood on their hands. And Castro, he knew, had jails full of those of "the people" who had made the mistake of disagreeing with their revolutionary hero. Suddenly, the fact that Henry Moore had a political conscience was not exactly a comfort.

A final picture caught Max's attention. It was a photo of a slightly younger Henry Moore with President Bill Clinton, whose arm was around Moore. "To Henry, Make a Difference! Good Luck, Bill Clinton," it was signed.

Noting his interest in the photo, Moore said, "I used to be a successful businessman in Detroit. But like many successful businessmen, I was empty inside. I had a deep inner void. I came to this island on vacation and I found myself deeply moved by the inequities and injustices suffered by the underprivileged classes. I was sitting on the beach drinking a—I don't know what I was drinking—but I experienced a revelation. I have been brought here on a sacred mission."

Max studied the man, trying to determine if he was sincere, and more importantly, how it tied in to having Max brought here at gunpoint. Max already had a pretty good idea about that, and though he hoped he was wrong, he rarely was.

"I began an outreach program to create an infrastructure to provide the essential social services that were sadly lacking for the poorer elements of society here," Moore added.

"And you want me to buy a table at your next fundraiser," Max offered.

Moore smiled and led him to a secured door at the back of the office. "No. Mr. Burdett, I'm offering you the opportunity to participate in the vital growth and provision of these social services."

"How's that?" Max asked.

"I want you to steal me the diamond," Moore said pleasantly.

There it was. Max was right. "I'm not a criminal," he said, keeping his tone casual.

"Right," Moore said quickly. "And neither am I."

"I'm glad we understand each other," Max said. What he did next, he did without thinking, his old reflexes and habits going to work. "You've got some lint there. May I?" he asked. Before Moore could respond, Max reached out toward the man's shoulder to brush it away, snapping off a stray thread in the process.

Moore buzzed them through the door, leading him

down a flight of stairs and into another part of the building. Max had seen a number of rooms like this before in many different parts of the world. What always amazed him was how alike they looked no matter where you went. There was always a demand for gambling, drugs, and hookers, and there were always rooms like this that provided them in a single convenient location.

The room was packed, with men huddled around roulette and blackjack tables, attractive prostitutes moving through the crowd with confidence. Money was changing hands, as well as packages that could be either drugs or guns or both.

"Let me ask you, Mr. Burdett. Do you think it's fair that those indigenous to this island aren't allowed to enter the casinos unless they work there? Why is it that only the rich get to enjoy pharmaceutically assisted moments of personal introspection, the pleasure of financially procured female companionship, and the joy of personal firearm ownership?" Moore asked.

"You mean gambling, drugs, prostitution, and guns," Max said.

"All I do, I do for the people. The underprivileged should not be denied these essential activities. Look around—no one is turned away. It's a very inclusive program. If you listen to the people, they'll tell you what they want."

There were plenty of "the people" in this room. For a moment, Max couldn't decide if Moore was a lunatic or a genius. "Why do you need the diamond for that?" Max asked, hoping to cut through this charade.

"I have an urgent need to expand my humanitarian

program. A cash injection in the tens of millions of dollars would alleviate the suffering of the underclass across the entire Caribbean," Moore said.

Max caught an unnerving sound, muffled, coming from an adjacent room. One of Moore's underprivileged "people" had no doubt gotten on the wrong side of his benefactor. "I am suggesting a partnership. You are a trained jewel remediator—but you are also a stranger to the island. I can give you what you don't have: access to the marina, the crews, rotation schedules, whatever you need. We would, of course, split the proceeds fifty-fifty."

It wasn't a bad deal, but Max never took on silent partners. He found that if people didn't share the risk, they didn't do their best work. And, of course, he *was* retired. His thoughts were disturbed by that noise again—this time it was even clearer. There was a cracking sound. Was it bones breaking? Then came a muffled scream.

"And if I say no?" Max asked.

Moore smiled pleasantly, as if they were having a casual conversation in which someone wasn't being tortured just a few feet away. "I'm a dignitary. An emissary. A man of the people. I do not make threats. What I am simply saying is that it would behoove you, on a deeply personal level, to cooperate with me on this enterprise. The people are relying on you."

Max had to fight to keep anything from showing on his face. Automatically, he scanned the room for exits and realized that there was no doorway that would get him out of the spot he was in now. "I wish you and your infrastructure well, Mr. Moore, but I can't help you. I've got no interest in the diamond."

Then the door to the adjacent room opened. A thug stepped out. Inside there was some kind of retribution under way. Moore's men were surrounding a bloodied, semiconscious man who was chained to the wall. Then the door closed.

"You have a unique way of demonstrating your love for the people," Max said.

"He's not the people," Moore replied, a hint of menace in his voice. Then the charming smile was back. As Max turned to leave, Moore said, "By the way, I love the view of the water from your house."

Of course, Moore could only have seen that view from inside his house. "You mean the view of my house from the water—" he corrected.

Moore flashed him a look and Max realized that the gangster had been inside his house, his and Lola's home. It was worse than having Agent Lloyd snooping around. This man was far more dangerous than Lloyd, who merely wanted Max in jail. Suddenly, Max felt like there was ten pounds of lead in his stomach.

"I mean what I said. Standing in your living room, looking at the ocean—it's peaceful tranquility. I'd hate to see that shattered."

There it was—Moore hadn't even bothered to veil the threat that time. Mustering a calm face, Max nodded to Moore and headed outside as quickly as he could. Up until now, he'd thought that stealing the diamond was foolish, tempting but too dangerous. Now he saw that not stealing it would be even more dangerous.

And even if he stole the diamond and got away with it *and* Moore let him and Lola live to keep their share, he would be connected to Moore in ways he did not want to contemplate. It was not easy to sever business ties with men like that, particularly when business was good.

Max knew he needed a plan, a way out, an angle he could play. For the moment, however, he was coming up completely blank.

Chapter Eight

Max rushed home. It was an irrational impulse. Moore had threatened him, but the man wanted something from him. He wouldn't try anything unless Max failed to do what he wanted. Lola would be safe until then. It all made perfect sense; nevertheless, he found himself pushing his car to get home faster.

When he arrived, he was relieved to see that nothing was amiss. Inhaling a deep breath, he took a moment to compose himself. Lola would pick up any sign, so he needed to be completely cool. To his surprise, he found himself relaxing, at least outwardly, as he did on a job. Inside, he was alert and ready for anything.

Inside the house, Lola was unpacking Chinese food. He forced himself to smile and said, "How's construction going?"

"Well. And did you find a hobby?" Lola asked. There was something forced in her own manner. Something was bothering her, Max realized.

"These things take time," he said.

Lola looked him over for a few seconds, seeming to look right through him. To his surprise, she simply said, "Really?"

They passed the evening quietly and went to bed without making love. Max realized that something new was bothering him. He wasn't being honest with her and he sensed that she was keeping a secret or two of her own.

Up until now, they had always been completely open with one another. Perhaps it was because of the way they made their livings, but Max had come to depend on that honesty. He depended on knowing that there was one person in the world who he could trust completely, one person around whom he could drop his own guard—defenses that were so deeply ingrained in him that he barely knew they were there.

He wouldn't be sleeping for a long time, if at all, tonight, so Max decided to get up and headed outside. In the back garden, he got onto the hammock and lay there, listening to the sound of the ocean and watching the water gently move in the dim light. Lola had found peace here. The beach, the ocean, him . . . they had been enough for her.

He had been restless and had only seen the things he was missing, not enough of the things that he had. Now that he might lose them all, Max realized that he was afraid, really afraid, for the first time in his career.

The sound of footsteps told him that Lola was coming, and he turned to see her approach. "I couldn't sleep. I didn't want to wake you," Max said.

"You gotta get out of your head, Max," Lola said, her tone serious.

"I like being in my head. It's the only place where I'm still the world's greatest jewel thief."

"I saw you on the ship yesterday," she said.

That explained a few things, including her mood since he had come home. "I had a feeling you'd be there too," he added.

Lola sat down next to him. She still smelled faintly of perfume and he took a moment to enjoy her warmth. "Don't you ever feel like we weren't quite finished? It was supposed to be a trilogy."

Shaking her head, Lola said, "So was *The Godfather*. Some things are best left at two. You reach for the third, you ruin what you had before."

"All an old fighter knows is to climb back into the ring," he said. He could see instantly that Lola wasn't buying it.

"And they get knocked out. It's called 'punch-drunk' for a reason. Look, Max, I miss it, too. We were great. We went out at the top of our game, undefeated. The best time to quit."

"Maybe," Max said. It was all he could think to say because he couldn't tell her what he was really thinking. He didn't want to burden her with the knowledge of Henry Moore's plans and his threats. If he played his

cards right, she wouldn't know about all that until the
danger was past. There was a solution out there; he
could feel it even if he couldn't see it yet. As he sat outside, Max wondered if his mind was keeping him awake
so it could work on the problem of how to get out of this
in one piece and stay out of jail.

"Well, I cased it. It's not a one-man job, and there's
no way you're pulling me into it. We're retired. Now the
challenge is to find joy in simple things. And I like that
challenge," she said.

"You're right," he said. She was, and she'd been very
patient with him, more than he probably deserved. He
came to a decision, and once he'd done that, he acted
immediately. Getting up, he grabbed the cordless phone
and dialed a number. After a few rings, a very groggy-
sounding Agent Lloyd picked up the other end.

"Hello," Agent Lloyd said.

"I lied on the ship. I could get it. Here's how: I'd cut
the camera feed and go in from behind the exhibit. It's
blowable from the storage room. And I'd do it after ten
p.m." he said.

"Why?" Lloyd replied.

"The arthritic retired cops always get that shift," he
said.

"So that's how you'd do it?" Lloyd said, a note of
confusion in his voice.

"And now I told you, so I can't," Max said. Imagin-
ing the look of surprise and disappointment on Lloyd's
face gave Max a rush of pleasure.

* * *

The next morning, at the marina, a seaplane landed gently on the ocean in the early light. It pulled up to a dock and almost immediately two very clean-cut men emerged wearing jeans and aviator sunglasses. Carrying a black duffel bag each, they scanned their surroundings professionally and then headed for the parking lot.

An empty cab stood waiting and they got inside, waking the driver. "Atlantis, please," one of the two men said.

Max woke to an odd smell that at first he couldn't place. He found Lola in the kitchen where she was . . . *cooking.* Lola was a world-class safecracker and a professional-caliber knife thrower; she could handle explosives like a Navy SEAL, and she was in the best physical condition of any partner he had ever worked with—but there were limits to her skills.

"What are you doing?" he asked, looking at the runny omelets that Lola was currently trying to flip.

"I'm cooking," she said innocently.

She might as well have said that she was taking up high-energy particle physics. "Since when?" he asked.

"This morning. We are decent, law-abiding people, and decent law-abiding people cook omelets for breakfast," she said.

Everything she said was true, but only for *other* decent law-abiding people. In some ways, he knew it was healthy for Lola to try new things, but a person had to know her limits. Looking at the state of their breakfast, he saw that Lola didn't know hers yet.

The phone rang and Max realized that there was no one he actually wanted to talk to. "State your business," he said.

"You almost had me last night with that old bunco trick," the voice said. As he suspected, it was Lloyd. Once again, he realized that he hated it when he was right. "Looky-looky at this hand, so I miss you filching my purse with the other."

"What are you on about?" Max said.

"I want to know how you're really gonna do it. And you're gonna tell me. When we're fishing," Stan said.

"Fishing? I don't fish," he said. The fact was that fishing was one of the things Lola had been bugging him to try. He hadn't done it yet for her; he'd be damned if he did it for Lloyd.

"I got a charger stacked with beer," Lloyd said.

Max realized he was in no mood. He had bigger problems—bigger fish to fry, as it were. "Drink it yourself. I'll pass," he said.

"It's not optional. It's general swim. Everybody in the pool," Stan said, waiting for Max to reply. When he didn't, Stan continued. "No, actually there is another option: I get the local police to bring you down to the station, we sweat you there. And I do mean sweat. There's no air-conditioning, so dress light."

Max didn't like being pressured into doing anything, and he didn't like it any better coming from Lloyd than he did from Moore. Maybe he would call Lloyd's bluff. Let them try to sweat him at the station. He hadn't committed any crimes on the island. As far as the local authorities were concerned, he was just another well-to-do private citizen in good standing—the kind that kept this island going.

Lola caught his attention and extended a piece of omelet on a fork. "The eggs on this island taste funny. They must have some weird chickens."

Tasting the eggs, Max hid his grimace. He made his next decision instantly. He might not like being pressured to do things, but perhaps Lola was right; perhaps it was time he tried new things.

"See you soon," he said into the phone.

"Lloyd?" Lola asked.

Max nodded. "They'll be less trouble if I talk to him in person. He's getting desperate," he said.

Lola nodded. "Can you stay for breakfast?" she asked.

"I'm afraid not," he said. "And it's better if I take care of this quickly."

Max kissed her and was out the door. At the marina, Lloyd was waiting for him and led him to a large fishing boat, at least forty feet in length. It was impressive, and suddenly Max was certain that Lloyd had charged it to his room at the Atlantis, which meant Max was footing the bill. Well, it was all a small price to pay to keep Lloyd off his back. On the deck, Stan handed him a beer and showed him to their poles.

Max decided that he might as well get comfortable and took off his shoes. As he rigged his fishing pole, Max flexed his left hand. It was numb again—nerve damage courtesy of Agent Lloyd.

"Tell me this isn't better than standing in some lineup," Stan said.

Max shrugged. "I've never been in a lineup."

* * *

The clean-cut man in the boat reached into his black duffel bag and pulled out his camera. Estimating the distance, he chose a telephoto lens and clicked it into place. Burdett and Lloyd were sitting on the deck of the fishing boat, and to his surprise they really seemed to be fishing, or at least going through the motions.

Raising the camera, he started snapping pictures.

Lloyd got some beers out of the ice chest and passed one to Max. As Max took the beer, Lloyd focused on his hand, on his wrist, and the Panerai watch he wore.

"That's some watch. What's that kind of thing run ya?" Stan asked.

"A few grand. Why don't you pick one up on the Bureau's expense account?" Max replied.

"They've got me on a real tight leash. I've got you to thank for that," Lloyd said.

That was interesting. Max wondered how much the loss of two of the three Napoleon diamonds to Max had cost Stan. They weren't the only things Max had taken out from under Lloyd's nose, but they were by far the most valuable. And though Lloyd had technically been in charge of security for the first diamond, he had not even known it was part of the exhibit. If there had been fallout, that blame would have been shared. Still, it must have hurt Lloyd professionally.

This was a new idea to Max. He had never kidded

himself—he was no Robin Hood. However, he had always made it a point, like John Robie in *To Catch a Thief,* to only steal from those who wouldn't go hungry. The fact was that he only took from the very richest people and organizations in the world. All of the pieces he acquired were insured; thus the only loser was a big insurance company who built losses like that into their business models. Max had always played to win, but he had taken some satisfaction in the fact that, in his game, there were no real losers.

Then he remembered the feeling he had looking at Lloyd struggling for breath in the SUV during the last job. Suddenly, Max understood that at least one person had paid a significant price for his success, that there was at least one loser in the game so far. Granted, Lloyd had shot him and nearly killed him—and more importantly, he could have killed Lola. Nevertheless, the fact was that Special Agent Lloyd did perhaps have his reasons for pursuing Max with such zeal. Max cast out his line and put the pole into the holder on the deck in front of him.

"Phew, it's cooking out here," Stan said.

It was. Max took off his shirt. Stan immediately eyed the bullet hole on Max's shoulder.

"So if I didn't shoot ya, where'd you get the screen door?" Lloyd asked.

"Knitting accident," Max said casually. He wouldn't be baited, not today.

"Uh huh," Lloyd said.

"You ever been shot?" Max asked him.

"Once in the shin," Lloyd said.

Max was mildly surprised, but realized he shouldn't have been. Stan had his own sort of nerve, the kind that would put him in harm's way from time to time. "Hurts, doesn't it," he said.

Stan nodded, "A lot."

Both men sat down in the folding chairs. Max took a sip from his beer.

"The profilers say miscreants are made during childhood," Lloyd offered.

"What can I say? I was abandoned. They left. I've always felt trapped by people, too many of them. That I could never trust anyone. That's what you want to hear? Sorry, I can't give you that."

Stan was looking at him with great interest, as if he was about to reveal something about himself. To his surprise, Max realized *he* was. "I was just another kid living in a row of houses that all looked the same. Nothing special. You?"

"Similar deal. Different continent," Stan said.

Well, they had something in common. A few somethings, Max realized. Of course, that didn't mean Max would play his hand any differently. He only had one speed: *On,* and he only played to win. In this case, he realized that he could win simply by staying out of the game. It would certainly deny Lloyd any kind of victory.

Stan rubbed sunscreen on his arms. Then he tried without much luck to put some on his back as well. After a few seconds, he said, "Can you put some on my back?"

"You serious?" Max said.

Stan shrugged. "I've got delicate skin. I don't want to burn," Lloyd said.

Taking the bottle, Max put some on his hands. It was the last thing he thought he'd be doing when he woke up this morning, but Max went ahead and rubbed the lotion onto Stan's back. In the end, he figured it was the least he could do, considering how often he had beaten the agent in the past. And the fact was, he wasn't done beating Lloyd.

"I bet you were the best in the neighborhood at hide-and-seek, so you joined the Bureau?" Max said.

"Yeah, I found 'em all," Stan said.

"No one ever found me. Sometimes when I got a good spot, I'd stay hidden for days," he replied.

Max finished applying the lotion. "Thanks. Turn around, I'll do you," Stan said.

"I'll handle it," Max said, realizing that Lola had usually done it. He tried and found that he simply couldn't reach the center of his back.

"You'll get burnt. Come on—" Stan said.

Max relented and Stan rubbed the lotion in. After a few seconds, Max said, "There, you got it all—"

"Not quite," Stan said, continuing.

There was movement nearby and Max looked over his shoulder at his fishing pole, which was bobbing in its holder. "My pole!" he said, feeling a rush of excitement.

Stan immediately misunderstood and raised his hands, saying, "No way, man, I'm just doing your back."

Ignoring him, Max lunged for his fishing pole, which was bowing seriously. He definitely had something on the line, and it was big. "I got something. Gimme a hand." Max dropped his beer in the excitement and he could see that Stan had done the same. Grabbing the handle on the reel, he started to pull whatever it was in.

"Come on, man. It's a shark," Stan said.

The pole was seriously dipping. Stan reached out a hand to steady it and said, "Holy shit," summing up what Max himself was thinking.

"Pull. Harder. Harder," Max said.

Max could see something break the top of the water for a moment and then disappear back down. With a final burst of energy, Max and Stan pulled together and the fish broke the surface. No, it wasn't a fish. It *was* a shark.

Pulling it on board the deck, Max realized that it was a tiger shark, about four feet in length. "Jesus Christ. It *is* a shark," Stan exclaimed.

"It's a shark! A shark!" Max parroted, feeling a rush of pride. The shark was lying on the deck motionless, and Max wondered if it was still dangerous. "Something's wrong. It's not moving," he said.

"Maybe it's in shock," Max said.

"Give me a beer. I'm going to throw a beer at its head to see if it's alive."

"No, no, no," Max replied.

"Well, what do we do?"

"It's dead," Max replied. "Well, I *think* it's dead. Just go over and shake it."

"Why me?" Stan asked.

"You're FBI."

"What's that have to do with anything?"

"If it bites your arm off, you get disability for the rest of your life. Go."

"You hooked it. You see if it's alive," Stan replied.

"Yeah, *I* hooked it. So *you* have to see if it's alive," he said.

Either Stan bought that argument or he was just getting impatient, because he started inching toward the shark.

"Okay—here I go," Stan said. Lowering his voice to a whisper, he added, "I'm gonna come around its back."

"Why are you whispering?" Max said.

"So it won't know the plan."

"I'm pretty sure it doesn't speak English."

As if it sensed he was closer, the creature suddenly came to life, writhing around in the boat, chomping its jaw hard.

Stan and Max jumped almost in unison, and Stan said, "Holy shit!"

"Watch out," Max said.

Panicking, Max looked frantically around the deck to find something—anything—to subdue the thrashing shark. Spying the ice cooler, Max snatched it up, raising it above his head and preparing to hurl it at the gnashing beast. Stan simply stepped forward with his service revolver, and aiming it at the shark, emptied the entire chamber into the shark's head.

"You have the right to remain silent," Stan quipped at the now limp shark.

"You're supposed to say that *before* you empty your clip," Max said. The two men stared at each other in disbelief of what had just transpired . . . then they both burst into laughter simultaneously.

"Man, I need a drink," Stan said.

"Or two!" Max added.

Reaching into the cooler, he pulled up two fresh beers and passed one to Stan. "Here. Cheers . . ." Max said. They clinked their bottles and each took a drink.

Lola had to stretch to reach the overhanging ceiling above the new deck. Still, it was satisfying work. She found that the liked the smell of the paint, the feeling of accomplishment as she put the finishing touches on the ceiling—the ceiling she had built above the deck she had built.

There was still some finishing work to do. The deck itself had to be stained and sealed, but it was nearly finished. Lola had learned a number of new skills to build this deck, but she picked up new things quickly. For jobs in the past, she had learned to do everything from typing to cutting hair to tightrope walking to knife throwing to high-level network programming. She had taken satisfaction in each new skill she had acquired and had taken even greater satisfaction when the job was finished and she he had *achieved* her objective.

Of course, the payoff had always been big. Now she was learning new things for herself, and for Max, since they would be married on this deck. The satisfaction was still there, she was pleased to see. There was only one skill that still eluded her: cooking. Well, they had plenty of time on this island. Time for each other, time to learn even the mysteries of the kitchen.

The island had been named Paradise, no doubt for the tourists. Nevertheless, she had found something real

Max Burdett,
burglar extraordinaire.

Max's partner in crime—
and in love—Lola Cirillo.

Max goes to work with cool nerves
and a steady hand.

Max and Lola celebrate their latest heist—
and the chance to start life anew.

Max and Lola find out that while life is good in Paradise, there can be some drawbacks—including the presence of law enforcement agencies on their tail.

Lola begins work constructing the
deck in preparation for the wedding.

Max and Stanley wrestle with their catch on a fishing trip.

Lola is concerned that Max is becoming too involved with
a scheme surrounding the Napoleon Diamond . . .

. . . despite Max's assertion that he has cleaned up his act
and is living the straight life.

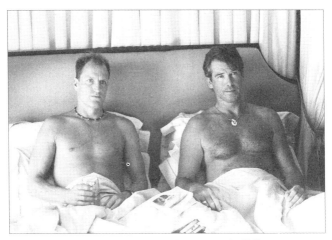

Circumstances often make the strangest bedfellows:
Max shacks up with Stan after Lola throws Max out of their house.

Henry Moore, the island "businessman" who makes Max
an offer he can't refuse.

Max stands up to Moore when confronted about the whereabouts of the diamond.

The loving couple reconcile.

Falling in love in Paradise is easy:
as Max and Lola finally exchange vows . . .

. . . Stan and island cop Sophie St. Vincent find out they share
much more in common than the law.

here, something like peace, something that they could build a life on. Max, she knew, was still searching. And she was prepared to wait for him. She only hoped it wouldn't be much longer. Looking out on the glittering ocean in front of her, she thought that it would be worth the wait for both of them.

She cleaned up quickly and decided to meet Max at the marina. Perhaps he had been able to accomplish something with Agent Lloyd. Stan was the last obstacle she could see to their life new together—the last obstacle besides Max's inability to make peace with retirement, at any rate.

At the marina, Lola saw a familiar face already waiting there. It was the policewoman, St. Vincent, who was leaning on the front of her car and watching the water. After pulling in beside her, Lola got out and leaned on the front of her car as well. Lola caught sight of Stan and Lloyd on the deck of one of the boats as it came in, and for a moment she and Sophie were just two women waiting for their men.

The two men looked to be in fine spirits. A dead shark was propped up on the deck, sitting in a fishing chair, wearing Stan's baseball cap. Stan and Max were singing an old sea shanty at the top of their lungs as they gathered up their gear.

"Look at 'em. If you didn't know better, you'd think they were friends," Lola said, watching the two tie up the boat and stagger down the pier carrying the cooler.

"You must be Lola," the policewoman said.

Lola smiled and nodded. "Sophie?" she said.

Sophie nodded and Lola realized she was very pretty,

pretty and exotic-looking, just Max's type back when he was still single. Then she noticed the pistol sitting on the woman's hip. "Nice gun. Sig Sauer P228?" she asked.

"Yeah. Custom trigger action," Sophie replied.

Then the woman looked her over for a few seconds, her gaze settling on Lola's feet. "Nice shoes. Manolo Blahnik, alligator?" Sophie asked.

"Yep. Summer collection," Lola replied.

The boat docked, Max and Stan working together to tie it up. She saw Lloyd trip as he got off the boat. Lola and Sophie shook their heads at the same time.

The illusion that this was a normal scene persisted until the men arrived. Then things became awkward. Whatever had transpired on the boat, back on shore Max and Lloyd were once again cop and criminal, hunter and prey. That didn't disturb Lola. Max was an unusual sort of prey—the kind that could turn and devour his predator.

Together, Max and Lola headed for her car. Inside she asked him, "How bad was it?"

"Not too bad," Max replied.

"Sophie seemed nice," Lola offered.

"For a cop," Max said.

"Lola's cool," Sophie said, as Lloyd got into her car. "For a thief," Stan responded immediately. He said it as a joke, but he meant it. Max and Lola were thieves, suspects that he planned to bring in. And besides that, they had cost him quite a bit on both a personal and a professional level.

Sophie was tough, but she was young and didn't automatically see all the dangers of this job. One of the worst mistakes you could make was identifying with your suspect. Understanding them was one thing—in fact, it was often necessary for catching them—but relating to them simply got in the way. It aroused sympathy, which affected your judgment and dulled your edge.

So even though Lloyd was able to spend a day out on a boat with Max and not shoot him, it didn't mean that when the time came he wouldn't arrest Max and savor every second of it.

Chapter Nine

Sitting over the Japanese go board, Max leaned in closer to Lola so their heads were nearly touching. He took a deep breath and enjoyed her scent.

"Hurry up and play your stone. I have to go and pick up the fish," Lola said.

Max looked down at the board. Already her white pieces were overtaking his black ones. "Just go now, you always win anyhow," he said.

"It's no fun if you quit this early," she said.

"We're almost at shukyoku. Even with a nine-stone okigo, I can never beat you," he said.

"Because your mind is always somewhere else," she

replied. With a sigh she put down a stone and suddenly her stones surrounded his.

Go had been invented in China thousands of years ago. The purpose of the game was to train military leaders. It was supposed to teach discipline, concentration, and balance as it showed officers how to overtake enemy territory and troops.

The game also had great depths and required great subtlety, particularly when both players were strong. Lola was probably good enough to play at the competition level. Max, however, wasn't nearly as good.

He had wondered about that once. The very skills that came easily to him in his work seemed to disappear when he played the game. Eventually, he understood what was missing for him in go: the stakes. A job always had a tangible reward at the end, and very real danger. He simply found it hard to remain engaged when there were no real stakes. When it was just a game, it was too much like a simulation—and a simulation, no matter how good, never came close to the real thing. There was no adrenaline, no edge. Max was never as engaged as he was during his work, which was a very real game with very real stakes.

Lola, however, was able to put her whole self into things, passionately, even when nothing was driving her but her own desire to try something new . . . or to play a game.

"I'm completely boxed in," he said, finally.

"There are always choices," she replied.

"Only if you can see a way out. I resign. You win, make a wish," he said.

"I wish you'd write your vows," she answered immediately.

She was right, of course. He had taken far too long—so long that even he began to doubt his excuses.

They started to put the stones away, Max dropped them into their wooden box. They fell one by one, making a thud as the stone hit the wood. And then one fell with a hollow click instead of a thud.

That was unusual. Hell, it was impossible.

In his suite, Stan sipped his beer inside the Jacuzzi. He found that he took pleasure in the fact that Max was paying for it all—the room, the beer, even the charter boat. It was, after all, the least Max could do considering their history.

Stan liked the idea that as he was bringing Max down he was doing it in style. Even now, he had his monitoring equipment nearby so he could listen to every word Max and Lola said. As usual, most of their conversations were boring domestic crap. What they were going to do, what they were going to eat, and the occasional strained discussion about their upcoming marriage. It was all routine, which Lloyd found disappointing in a way.

With all of their money, Lloyd had expected their lives would be bigger, better, more interesting somehow. Instead, they lived like most people he knew, only they lived in a nicer house, drove nicer cars, and played fancier board games—even as the hour-to-hour, minute-to-minute details of their lives were excruciatingly ordinary.

"Come here, baby. I have a consolation prize for you," Lola's voice said through the speaker. She'd lowered her voice, making it huskier. Stan sat up. Suddenly, things were getting more interesting.

Then he could clearly hear the sounds of kissing—heavy kissing. "Now we're talking," Stan said, leaning in and putting up the volume a little.

"Mmm," Lola's voice said.

"Oh yeah," Stan said to himself. Lola was attractive. Hell, she was beautiful, and Stan had wondered a few things about her. In a few minutes, he realized that all of his questions would be answered.

Then there was the sound of a doorbell ringing.

"Are we expecting anyone?" Max's voice said.

"I've got a surprise for you. I've asked a new friend over," Lola said, her voice just above a purr.

Stan took back everything he'd thought about these two living an ordinary life. Maybe the rich really were different. Maybe Max's life was about to turn into one big, late-night, made-for-cable movie. *Lucky son of a bitch,* Stan thought. He heard footsteps and then Max said, "What is she going to do?"

"Tell him," Stan said.

"She's going to help me relax you." Lola said.

Stan's breath caught in his chest. He took a sip of his beer and then he heard Max say, "Max, I'd like you to meet Mrs. Carol Lloyd—Stan's mother."

Stan jumped and choked on his beer. *What the hell?* he thought.

Then there was another sound that, at first, Stan could not place. It sounded like water moving, followed by a roar. It didn't make any sense . . . until it did.

Max and Lola had found his bug, and had just flushed it down the toilet.

Son of a bitch, Lloyd thought.

When they finally stopped laughing, Lola smiled at Max and said, "Finally, we've got Stan out of our house."

Max nodded. That was how it felt. Since he'd seen Agent Lloyd in his living room, he had not been able to relax in his own home knowing that Lloyd was listening to their every word and move. As a result, they hadn't made love nearly enough. Well, it was time to change that.

"I can think of a perfect way to celebrate," he said to Lola before he kissed her.

After the kiss, she pulled back and said, "I like the way you think."

As they headed for the bedroom, he said, "About my greatest fantasy . . ."

"Mr. Burdett, I'm shocked. That was for Lloyd's benefit," she said.

"Of course, but since you brought it up," he said.

"I tell you what—when I'm finished with you, if you still have enough energy, we'll talk about it," she said.

Max smiled at that. It was going to be a long night, if he was lucky.

* * *

Hours later, the thief watched the parking lot at the docks carefully. He had studied the movements there well enough to know that he would not have to wait long. Sure enough, after a few minutes the man he was waiting for appeared. A cleaning person dressed in a white uniform and cap got out of his car and headed for the cruise ship.

The thief waited behind a cargo container until the cleaning man stepped near. When the thief moved, he moved very quickly. The cleaner barely had time to register the movement nearby before he felt a chloroform-dipped cloth cover his mouth. Unconscious in seconds, the cleaning man went limp in the thief's hands.

Pulling the man far out of sight, the thief went to work quickly. Less than two minutes later, he was wearing the cleaning man's clothes—a good fit, the thief had done his homework on this one. He made his way to the ship casually, carrying his bucket and cleaning supplies, adopting a good approximation of the cleaning man's walk as he moved.

He took the ramp up to the ship and made his way to the sky deck where a good number of passengers were still awake, cavorting in the Jacuzzi, drinking champagne, and making out. Keeping his distance from the passengers, the thief swept the deck, keeping a careful eye around him.

After a few minutes, he headed below deck. He found the ship's engineer's office. The door, of course, was locked, but the thief reached a gloved hand into his belt and pulled out a locksmith pick set that was a folding, self-contained unit that looked like a Swiss Army knife. The set was nickel-plated and made according to his own specifications. The picks were also manual—as the thief eschewed the new electric picks. In skilled hands, a manual pick was faster and it was certainly quieter, which was essential in his work.

The lock on the door had a narrow keyway so it took him a full minute to open. Then he was inside the office and quickly found what he was looking for. He found all of the diagrams and schematics he needed in a single cabinet. Laying them out on the table, the thief quickly took pictures of them with a high-resolution digital camera, though he would remember most of the basics from his quick study of the material.

Stan scanned the security monitors. They showed the entire ship, including the gem exhibit room. The system, like the ship, was top-notch and state-of-the-art. It also wouldn't mean a damn thing if Burdett was determined to get the diamonds. That was fine with Stan; he knew that it would take more than equipment—even good equipment—to put Max away. It would take the human factor, judgment, and intuition. Stan would have to be on his game. That was fine; he had never felt more ready—and he'd never had so much riding on a single case.

His job now was to watch carefully and wait for Burdett to make a mistake. He'd only made one on the last job, and that one had almost been enough. It had allowed Stan to put a bullet into Max's shoulder. Stan had done what was necessary then and he was prepared to do the same thing again when the time came.

Sophie stood next to him, watching the monitors as well. Stan had to admit that partnering with her had improved his chances of closing this case. It was easier for local police to get access to ship and dock security than it was for an American FBI agent with no jurisdiction out here. And without her, he doubted that he would have ever gotten into the ship's surveillance room.

Satisfied for now, he turned to the security chief and said, "You're only in port for forty-eight more hours. Stay on high alert."

"We have the most extensive security system ever installed on a seagoing vessel," the chief said, his voice and face radiating absolute confidence. For a moment, Stan considered trying to explain what they were up against to the chief, but he didn't bother. Some things you didn't believe until you experienced them for yourself.

Ultimately, the security team, like the expensive electronics, was simply a tool. This game was between Max and him. The most Stan could hope for was that the chief would do his job competently and that Stan would be there when things started to go to hell. And now that Max had found his listening device, Stan knew that his best chance was to stay with the diamonds as much as he could in the next two days.

Suddenly, a phone rang and a red light lit up on the security board. The chief answered it himself and hung up. "What is it?" Stan asked.

The chief shrugged and said, "They found someone passed out on the docks. Probably a drunk tourist."

Immediately alert, Stan said, "Anything unusual about him?"

The chief smiled and said, "Well, he was in his underwear."

"Sound the alarm," Stan said. "Burdett is on board."

"What?" the chief said, incredulous. "A drunk, we get them all the time."

"I guarantee you that when you check, you will find that the 'drunk' works on this ship. He's either maintenance or cleaning crew. That's why his clothes are gone and that's how Burdett is moving around on board this ship."

The chief looked confused, looking from Stan to Sophie. "It doesn't make any—"

"But that's what's going on," Sophie interjected. "Sound the alarm."

"Okay," the chief said, holding up his hands. "I'll check it out." Clearly he wasn't convinced, but he wasn't going to put up any more fuss. That was fine, Stan just needed him to do his job. The chief hit a button on the board. Immediately, an alarm sounded. Then he hit another button and leaned down to speak into the microphone. "We got a suspect on board. I want a full-team sweep of every deck. Check all maintenance and cleaning crews against their photos. Now. And double up the men on the exhibit."

"How long will that take?" Sophie asked.

The chief shrugged. "Grab a cup of coffee, it's a big ship," he said.

"Do you think he's making a move on the diamonds?" Sophie asked.

"No, not yet," Stan said.

"Then I have an idea about where he might be," Sophie asked. A few minutes later, they were at the engineer's office and the security chief was hurrying to open it. The chief was starting to sweat. *Good,* thought Stan. He had reason to sweat. *Thirty million good reasons.*

Inside the office, Stan asked, "Anything disturbed?"

"I think some schematics are missing," the chief said.

"You think it was Max?" Sophie asked.

"Absolutely," Stan said.

"Then he's trying to get off the ship," Sophie said.

"Impossible. The exits were shut when the alarm sounded," the chief said.

Stan shook his head. "Main deck," he said to Sophie, who nodded and was first out the door.

The thief heard the alarm and walked the last flight of stairs to the main deck. He took them slowly, making sure he looked completely normal to anyone who might see him. A few seconds later, he found what he was looking for. Opening the laundry room door, he removed the cleaning man's uniform and threw it onto a pile of dirty laundry. Underneath, he was wearing his black clothing. From his pocket he removed a black mask and pulled it over his face. The alarm had been a surprise, but his movements betrayed no nervousness.

* * *

Stan and Sophie split up and Stan searched the small crowd near the golfing net for Burdett. Max wasn't there. Next, Stan checked the railings on both sides of the ship to see if Burdett was trying to climb down to the water. Nothing.

Then he saw something, a dark figure moving in the shadows one deck below him. He ran inside, looking for a way down. After finally finding a staircase, he took the stairs two at a time, when suddenly he heard Sophie shout, "Don't move!"

Stan leaped down the remaining half dozen steps and burst through the nearest door. There were two figures just outside the door. Spinning right, he found himself face-to-face with Sophie's gun. The frustration was plain on Sophie's face, which meant Burdett was behind Stan and Stan was blocking her shot.

Stan swung his body around to grab Burdett and turned just in time to see a gloved fist coming straight for him out of the shadows. Taking it full in the face, Stan felt himself going down. From the ground, he saw a black-clad figure step up on the railing and take a swan dive straight down into the water.

Getting up quickly, Stan thought, *I've got you.* Burdett wouldn't be able to move very quickly in the water. Security would get him before he could get to land. Watching the figure fly through the air, Stan saw him suddenly produce a short length of rope, which he swung around the ship's mooring line.

No! Stan thought.

Suddenly, the figure was riding the mooring cable

like a zip line, straight to the dock. He hit the ground gracefully, and ran off, almost immediately disappearing into the darkness.

"Suddenly we're chasing Cirque Du Soleil," Stan said.

L ola paid for the fish at the market. She had a new recipe for broiling tuna and was determined to make it work. As soon as she left the market, she heard an alarm. Tracking the sound, she realized that it was coming from the direction of the docks. No, not the docks, the ship.

Max is going after the diamond, was her first thought. Then she dismissed it. Not because she put it past her fiancé but because she was almost certain that he hadn't had enough prep time. Still, something was going on and it was hard to imagine that he wasn't somehow involved. There was only a handful of people in the world who could even make an attempt at the diamond, and fewer still who had a chance of success.

She, of course, was one of them, and so was Max. Jumping into her car, she saw cops and security swarming around the cruise ship. If Max was involved, she hoped that he'd gotten away clean so she could kill him.

Lola raced toward home and was in the driveway a few minutes later. She changed quickly into a nightgown and found Max lying in the tub, a glass of Jack Daniels in his hand, a small notebook sitting on the tub's ledge by his other hand. She watched him from the doorway for a few moments before speaking.

"You're cheating on me, aren't you?" she asked, a smile playing on her lips.

"What are you talking about?" Max asked, disoriented.

"You think about her all the time," Lola said. "You even dream about her, don't you, Max?"

"Lola, I am *not* cheating,"

"Maybe not with another woman. But with a diamond. You want her, Max, we both know it. And I'm jealous."

Max looked at her earnestly. "You have nothing to worry about," he said.

"Where were you tonight?"

"I've been home," Max replied, picking up the notebook by the tub. "Writing my vows."

"Let me see." Lola moved toward him, but before she could reach the edge, Max quickly dropped the notebook into a black bag resting on the floor near the tub.

"Sorry," he said slyly, "you'll just have to wait."

"I'm not gonna let that little bitch take my man," Lola said, defiantly. "I'm going to fight for what's mine."

"And how exactly are you going to do that?"

With a coy look, Lola traced her arm with her fingertips, moving her hand toward the thin strap of her nightgown and slowly sliding it off of her shoulder, seductively letting it drop to the side. "I'm a thief—I know a thing or two about distractions."

Max was certainly distracted, sitting upright now in the tub, watching as Lola peeled the other strap down her shoulder.

"It's a beautiful jewel, Max," Lola purred, her gown falling to the floor, "but I guarantee you, it's no fun in the tub."

Max could not contain himself, and grabbed at Lola, the two of them falling into a passionate embrace as they spilled back into the tub, the glass of Jack Daniels shattering on the tile beside Max's black bag.

With flashlights, Stan and Sophie examined the spot where the half-naked cleaning man had been found. Stan peered around cargo containers and equipment, but nothing was out of place. *Max wouldn't leave any signs behind,* Stan thought. Of course, there was no proof that Burdett was involved, but Stan didn't need proof; he knew.

"What is wrong with you, Agent Lloyd? I had him— you should have stayed out of my way."

"I didn't want you to get hurt," Stan replied, rubbing his sore cheek. "I'm sorry."

"You're the one who's hurt. You should ice that," Sophie said, pointing to the spot where the suspect had hit him. "Why are men always trying to protect women?"

"Because you smell good."

Sophie rolled her eyes. "It's all about sex, isn't it? Why can't we just be two cops working a case?"

"I agree. From now on, we're just partners on this."

"Fine."

"So, you want to go for a Jacuzzi, partner? I've got a big tub in my room."

Sophie smiled resignedly, shook her head and walked away.

"How about a steam?" Stan called out hopefully after her. "I always take steams with my partners. Let's have dinner and discuss it."

Suddenly, one of the local cops called out and said, "Hey. We got something. Clothing fibers."

That got Stan's attention. Perhaps Max had made another mistake. Perhaps retirement had made him soft. Or perhaps Stan had just gotten very, very lucky. Whatever the reason, it was the first good news he'd had on this case. He'd take it.

"I'll bet they'll match something of Max Burdett's," she said.

L ola turned around to walk outside. Once there, she realized there was something she could do, and it would certainly feel better than standing around waiting for herself to calm down. Getting back into the car, she headed for the marina. The area had been cordoned off and police were moving around with a purpose—which meant they hadn't yet caught their suspect.

Nearby in the crowd, Lola saw two very clean-cut men. They had short, neat hair, serious expressions, and painfully straight postures. They were also wearing garish tourist clothes that they did not look comfortable in. Almost certainly American, she guessed they were military or federal agents. Were they working with Stan?

She doubted it, but she had a hunch that they were here for the same reason he was. They were looking around alertly, and one of them jotted something down in his notebook.

Then again, they could simply be tourists. Perhaps she was seeing things, jumping at shadows. She had hoped to come here and feel better, but she had found no comfort. Lola would have preferred to see that the police had a suspect in custody, but no such luck.

As she turned to go, she heard someone call her name. Sophie and Stan approached her, their faces dead serious. "We'd like to have a talk with Max," Stan said.

"Of course you would," Lola replied.

"Officially," Stan said.

"Then of course you'll have a warrant, particularly if you want to search the house," Lola said.

Stan muttered something under his breath but Sophie calmed him with a hand on his shoulder. "We'll see you in a few hours, with a warrant," she said to Lola.

Lola went home where Max was already asleep. Lola joined him. She gave him a shake and told him they would have company in the morning. They both woke up early, not wanting to be awoken by the police.

Max had breakfast started before she could even offer to make it, and then he went outside. It was only a few minutes later that Lloyd and Sophie arrived at the door. Lloyd held up the warrant, then said hello. Lola nodded and took them around back. Max was sitting on the small pier, looking as relaxed as an innocent man—or as relaxed as Max pretending to be an innocent man.

Max held up his homemade fishing pole and said, "See this? You created a monster." Lola noticed that the dexterity in his left hand was improving.

"They've got a warrant for the house," Lola said.

"I'm sure you heard someone stole the boat's schematics last night. Sounds like your MO," Stan said.

"Wasn't me," Max said affably. Lola could see that Max was baiting Stan.

"You wouldn't lie to your old fishing buddy, would you?" Stan shot back.

"Only if I were a thief," Max replied.

Listening to them, Lola realized that they both enjoyed the game they were playing with each other. Despite the fact that Max had been shot and that Stan had been, at the very least, heavily embarrassed, they were *enjoying* this. Sophie was watching them with a look of disapproval, as if she were thinking the same thing as Lola. Finally, Sophie headed back toward the house.

"I'm starting the search. I'm taking fiber samples of all garments," Sophie announced.

"Suit yourself, but it wasn't him," Lola said.

"What makes you so sure? His word that good?" she asked.

"He told me, and his word is gold . . ." Lola said, realizing that she meant it. Sophie gave a slight shrug and continued toward the house. Lola went with her.

She could hear the men still talking. "The ship's leaving dock for its last two nights, as a precaution. It's going to be anchored out in the harbor."

Lola shook her head. That was exactly the kind of thing that would scare off most thieves—and make Max *more* interested. Of course, she realized that might be Stan's intention.

"You think that'll scare the guy?" Max asked.

"Make it tougher for him," Stan replied.

Lola turned to look at Max's response. He only smiled, looked at Stan, studying the bruise on his cheek and said, "You should ice that."

Inside, Sophie was respectful of their things and was surprisingly quick. Mostly, she seemed interested in Max's clothing. Stan poked around in other parts of the house, but Lola could see that he was just killing time. Clearly, they had some fibers from the crime scene that they were hoping would match Max's clothes.

Not likely, Lola thought, even if Max had been there. Still, Lola couldn't blame them for trying. When they finally left, Lola plugged in her extension cord and got her electric sander.

Max watched Lola working hard in the hot sun. She was running her sander, which looked too big for a woman her size and out of place in the hands of a woman as beautiful as she. Nevertheless, she was toiling, working devoutly in preparation for their wedding—their life together.

While Max had been struggling with himself and his childish attempts to adjust to life in paradise, she had been building something, for them . . . He decided that he'd had enough. This game, this farce had to end here. Once the decision was made, Max found that he felt more relaxed than he'd felt in weeks.

Of course, there was still the little matter of Henry Moore. Their meeting wouldn't be easy, but the stakes were high and Max was at his best when the stakes were highest.

Chapter Ten

This time, as Max drove through the seamy side of Paradise Island, he had one thought. *This is bad, but Moore wants to make it much worse.* As if poverty, little or no education, and a dim future weren't enough trouble for these people, Henry Moore wanted to bring them gambling, prostitution, drugs, and guns—all in the name of social equality.

Max pulled up next to Moore's building to find Moore outside with a small group of gorgeous mixed-race young women who were piling into his limo. Well, Moore's prostitutes were certainly diverse. And Max had no doubt that Moore treated them all equally.

Disappointed, Max saw that the girls would make it difficult for the two of them to talk, assuming Moore was even willing since he seemed to have a previous engagement—a number of them, actually. Still, Max was determined to try. He got out of his car, approached Moore, and said, "We have to talk."

"Max, good, in a moment. Ride with us," Moore said.

Female hands pulled Max inside the limousine. Half a dozen perfumes competed for his nose while bare flesh from half a dozen girls competed for his eyes. Max kept his gaze on Moore, who was sitting across from him. Moore was smiling, no doubt enjoying Max's discomfort. "Are you familiar with the pleasures of anonymous love, Max?"

"No, I'm not," he said.

"Recently, I have found myself experimenting with alternative lifestyle parameters based largely on the free love philosophy found in the collected works of The Mamas & The Papas," Moore said.

Whatever was going on in this limo, Max thought, it wasn't love and it certainly wasn't free. "I never made the connection," was all he said.

"Oh, it's there. Whoo, that Michelle Phillips could walk it like she talked it. Mmm." Moore leaned forward to address the driver. "Earl, burn one of my CDs for Max."

On the way, Max was pleased to see the girls had no real interest in him. Moore was no doubt paying the bills and they were obviously trying to keep him happy. After a few minutes, the limo pulled up to a construction site and the girls piled out. Moore and Max followed.

The site was large and obviously in the beginning stages of construction. Destruction, actually, Max realized. Bulldozers were taking out the remnants of a large brick building as a large mulching machine turned felled trees into pulp. In one swoop, Moore was getting rid of the island's nature *and* history. Somehow, it all fit perfectly.

"This is my vision—my infrastructure—growing before our eyes. A former children's hospital that I am revitalizing into a gentleman's club," Moore said.

So, Max thought, *it's even worse than I thought.*

"More importantly, the ship is leaving in two days," Moore said, his voice losing its expansive, friendly air. He studied Max for a moment, waiting.

Max didn't hesitate and handed Moore the envelope. "Here's everything you need: the schematics and a detailed plan," he said.

From the expression on Moore's face, Max might have just as well handed him a baby blanket. "Why are you giving this to me?" he asked.

"Because I'm out. Finished," Max said, his tone final.

Suddenly, Moore's face went grim. His eyes flicked to the nearby machine. The mulcher destroyed a medium-size tree, turning it into pulp. "You know, I'm not a violent man, but I have never really grown accustomed to the word 'no.'"

Max found that he was not the least bit intimidated. Rather, he was angry. He kept himself in check and when he spoke he made sure that Moore understood he was serious. "Look, I'm done pulling jobs. You want to mulch me, go ahead."

Clenching his jaw, Moore said, "Walk me through the plan."

That was it. Moore wanted to kill him, that much was very clear—but he wanted the diamond more.

Max took back the envelope as Moore called Jean-Paul over. On the hood of the limo, Max laid out the ship's schematics. He pointed out relevant details as he spoke. "Go in through the air-conditioning vents. The exhibit is accessible from the storage facility behind it. There are cameras there, so you need to cut the central feed—the red wires in the control panel here. If you don't cut the red wires, they'll see everything."

"What next?" Moore asked.

"Then blow the wall," Max said simply.

"C4?" Moore asked.

"I'd use a shape-charge with a detonation cord. It's smaller but more effective," Max said. Actually, Lola would probably have handled that. She was much better with explosives than Max himself. For a moment he found himself wishing he and his fiancée were working this job together. Shaking off the thought, he continued, "And you'd want to blow it after ten p.m."

"Why?" Moore asked.

"Graveyard shift. Always the retired cops with arthritis," Max explained. Then he folded up the plans. "And that's how I'd do it," he said.

Moore took the plans from him. "You know we're not equal partners anymore. In fact, you see me, cross the street."

Max nodded. And that was it. He was free, of Moore

at least. Of course, he still had a few things to take care of before he was completely out of the woods, but he felt like a huge weight had been lifted off of him.

Moore had some business at the construction site and stayed with the women. Earl, the chauffeur, took him back to his car and handed him a small envelope when he got out of the limousine.

"What?" Max said, opening the envelope and finding a CD.

"The Mamas & The Papas," Earl said. "It's in chronological order. I, for one, prefer the earlier material, but you decide."

"Thanks," Max said, getting into his car. As he drove away, he popped the music on. The CD began with "California Dreamin'," followed by "Monday, Monday." Both from their first album. The driver was right, the earlier stuff *was* better.

When he reached the large Centerville Park, Max picked up his cell phone and dialed. "Mr. Lloyd, the Bridge Suite please," he said.

"Yallo?" Stan's voice said over the phone.

"It's Max. Checking in," he said.

"Cut the crap. You're making sure I'm in my room and not following you," he said.

"How could you be following me if you're in your room? See you soon, Stanley," he said.

Max turned the phone off and waited. The next move was Stan's.

* * *

Lola was relaxing at home, and decided to do some stretching to loosen up. Lying on her back on the bedroom floor, she fluidly moved from one Yoga position to another, letting her tense muscles relax. But just as she was letting her mind empty of stress and worry, her eyes caught sight of a familiar object underneath the bed—Max's black bag, the one that he had in the bathroom the night he spent soaking in the tub, writing his vows.

Lola snatched the bag and opened it up, reaching in to take out the little notebook. A wave of guilt washed over her inquisitiveness—she was sure Max wanted to keep his vows a secret until the day he uttered them at their wedding. Feeling guilty at the invasion, Lola set the book down and was about to lie back down and continue stretching . . . but her curiosity got the better of her.

She picked up the notebook again, and began flipping though the pages. One after the other, they were all blank, devoid of writing—no grand statements of his everlasting ardor for her, no solemn declarations of love, honor, and cherishment until the day they died. Fighting back both her rage and the tears, Lola carefully replaced the notebook back in the bag and shoved it back beneath the bed.

From his car, Stan watched Max's car in the distance. "I love call forwarding," he said to himself. Max's yellow Camaro stuck out like a sore thumb on this island. Whereas Stan only rented nondescript vehicles and kept changing them so Max couldn't spot him.

The Camaro made a turn. Stan waited a few seconds

and followed. Max was a smug bastard, but his pride would do him in. They approached the Centerville Park now and Max stopped his car, jumping out. A safe distance away, Stan did the same.

Burdett entered the park where at least a hundred Junkanoo musicians were milling around, playing in small groups. They were dancing, playing drums and all sorts of brass instruments, some of which Stan recognized and some he did not.

Though it was crowded, the musicians made room for Max, and for a moment, Stan had the uncanny feeling that Max knew them somehow. Following, Stan waded through the crowd, which wouldn't move for him at all. In fact, they seemed to be going out of their way to bump into him.

He felt a series of elbows and shoulder bumps as Max surged ahead and out of sight. When his cell phone rang, it took Stan a few seconds to reach it in the crowd. Then Max was on the line, saying, "If you're going to forward your calls, don't tail me so close."

Cursing under his breath, Stan pushed forward, but the crowd was making it harder for him. He'd had it. These people were working with Max, and they were not only messing with him, they were interfering with an investigation. Turning right, he found himself facing a trombone slide that hit him in the chest and knocked him flat to the ground.

Now he wasn't just angry. He was furious. Jumping up, Stan shoved the trombone player back. As the musician fell into someone else, someone pushed at Stan from behind.

Then from the side.

And then the *other* side. Stan turned to take a swing at somebody, when someone else hit him in the ribs. Another musician hit him in the stomach. And then the ribs again. Finally, he saw a fist flying toward his face. Before he could duck or lift a hand to deflect, he felt the fist make contact with his nose. Seeing stars, Stan went down.

Things seemed to go quiet around him. Stan shook his head and saw that the musicians were moving away, apparently having lost interest in him. *Because Max has gotten away,* he realized.

Feeling blood run down from his nose, Stan started to get up. Someone was in front of him: Sophie. She handed him a tissue and said, "Charming some more of the locals, Agent Lloyd?" She pointed to the musicians, who were now twenty yards away. "Which one hit you?" she asked.

"All of them," Stan said. Then he shrugged and said, "Forget them. Max got away."

An ambulance arrived and Sophie said. "I saw you get into trouble and called it in. Do you think it's broken?" she said, gesturing to his nose.

"No, but it hurts like a son of a bitch," he said. Then a medic arrived with a stretcher and Stan said, "I don't need that."

"Let him take a look—there's no rush now," Sophie said, then headed off to talk on her phone.

Stan shrugged and sat on the side of the stretcher. The medic prodded and poked him for a minute and said, "It's not broken, but I bet it hurts."

"That your medical opinion?" Stan said.

"No charge," the medic said, handing him a cloth. "Hold this over it until the bleeding stops."

Finished, Stan got up and the medic packed up the stretcher, putting it back into the ambulance. Sophie walked back over and said, "The fibers came back negative. No match for Max."

"Maybe he *is* retired," Stan said, trying out the thought for the very first time.

"I doubt it. He met with Henry Moore today. The biggest gangster on the island. Something's up," she said.

"Thanks for coming," he said, realizing that he meant it.

She smiled at him. The first genuine smile he had seen on her face since they met. Sophie did have a nice smile, he saw. And this one was for him.

"You okay?" she asked.

"I got hit by a trombone. And then a lot of fists," he said.

Pointing to his nose, she said, "This one you really have to ice."

Reaching out, she gently touched the bridge of his nose. Stan flinched, which seemed to amuse her. Then she leaned forward and planted a kiss on the spot. "Better?" she asked.

For the first time, Stan realized how big her eyes were, and how pretty. Stan had always seen her as attractive, but her looks had always been tempered by her toughness. But she was also soft, if you knew where to look—if you looked in her eyes.

"There's another one here," Stan pointed to his cheek. She kissed it.

"Now?" she asked.

"This one's particularly painful," he said, pointing to his neck. There was another kiss.

Then he pointed to the area around his lips. "I have some more pain somewhere around here," he said. This time, as she moved in to kiss him, he gently turned his face and kissed her on the lips. Her lips were incredibly soft, and warm. "I'm going to have to get hurt more often," he said.

"And in more interesting places," she said. Stan's breath caught in his throat for a moment. He leaned in to kiss her again. This time, he didn't hold anything back and neither did she.

Back in Stan's suite, Sophie and Stan fell into each other's arms, then tumbled into bed, frantically trying to remove each other's clothing. As they passionately kissed, Stan knew that everything was perfect to accentuate the mood: seductive music softly played from the stereo, and he had caviar and a bottle of chilled champagne brought to the room.

Sophie began to remove her shirt while Stan tried to unwind his head bandage in the sexiest way he could muster. Suddenly, Sophie's face dropped.

"Oh God . . . I'm vibrating."

"So am I," Stan crooned. "Just go with it."

"No, I'm getting a call." Sophie reached into her pants pocket and withdrew her cell. Putting it up to her ear, she listened to the voice on the other end as it relayed terse instructions, then she put the phone back in her pocket.

"Shit. I have to go."

"Go? No, you can't go! I just unwrapped my head!" Stan complained.

"Sorry. I need a rain check."

"Are you crazy? It never rains here. Just give me ten minutes," Stan begged.

"I don't have ten minutes."

"Then give me seven minutes. I'm begging you for seven minutes."

Sophie stood up. "Four minutes. Best I can do."

"Six?" Stan pleaded.

Sophie looked at him, his bandage half unraveled, the pathetic look on his face. It was actually endearing. "Five."

Stan grinned broadly. "Deal."

Max made his way through the park and doubled back around to his car. From a distance he could see a scuffle breaking out, with Stan right in the middle of it. He hopped into the Camaro and drove to the next town, where he pulled up to Sourire Soleil and Voile. It was exactly what he was looking for, an off-the-beaten-path scuba and boat rental store nestled in a remote area. It was the perfect place for Max to pick up a new skill and to get himself one step closer to real freedom.

Max was busy checking out a retractable fishing rod when his cell phone rang. Instinctively, he answered it.

The voice on the other line was Luc, the bartender at the tiki bar. "Mr. Burdett, there's a guest down here that is bombed and shouting your name," Luc said. There was noise on the other side—Max could clearly hear Stan yelling out "Welcome to paradise, right? Well, it's only paradise for criminals like Max Burdett!"

Sighing, Max said, "I hear him. I'll be right there."

He hopped into the Camaro and made his way to the tiki bar. He saw Stan at the bar with Luc behind it. Max watched Stan lift up a cocktail and down it in one long gulp. He approached and tried to pull the glass out of Stan's hand. At first Lloyd wouldn't let go; then he did and slumped back in his chair, completely hammered.

"What're you doing to yourself? What's wrong?" he said.

"Nothing," Stan replied.

"Nothing's wrong?" Max repeated. For a moment, it felt like he was talking to Lola.

"Exactly. Every time things are going good, that's when you screw me up. I was about to be made field office chief, then you took Napoleon I. I finally got some cred back, then you shoved Napoleon II up my—"

"And now?" Max said.

"We got together. Me and Sophie. We hooked up," he said.

"Why?" Max asked. This was getting interesting, a development he hadn't planned for.

"Because the ship's only here for twenty-four more hours and you're gonna clip Napoleon III and make me look like a jerk again." Stan slurped at his nearly empty glass. "Things just don't work out for guys like me. I may

160

as well go and get 'Born to Lose' tattooed on my forehead. Only with my luck, the guy'd be looking in a mirror and do it backward. People'd say 'Here comes Stan, he's *dorn* to lose.'" Looking up to Luc, Stan said, "Gimme another here."

"You've had enough," Max said. Then he noticed something about the glass in Stan's hand. "I didn't have you as an umbrella sort of guy."

"These Remoras have got a kick to 'em," Stan said, sipping the last of it.

"C'mon, Stan, buck up," Max said, realizing that he actually felt sympathy for him.

"You know what it's like, man, to be an ox? I'm just an ox. A dumb ox," he said.

"Stan—" Max started.

"No, no. I know the truth. Just yoke me up and let me plow along," Stan said.

"Don't beat yourself up, you're a good agent," Max said. He noticed that Luc had just shown up behind the bar, looking like he had recently put on his uniform.

"I used to blame you, but now I see it clearly. It's not you, it's me. You've got genius. I'm just a grunt. Man, if I had an ounce of what you have, I'd never stop. You've got a gift, man. It's inspiring," he said. Stan looked up at Luc and said, "Get me another Remora . . ." Then he ran out of steam and slumped onto the table.

"Luc, a little help here," he said.

Max and Luc put their arms around Stan and dragged him away from the bar. Agent Lloyd was nearly dead weight and moving him was a struggle. So was stuffing him into the Camaro and getting him out again. Finally, they dragged him through the lobby of the Atlantis and to the elevator.

"You always get your customers this juiced up?" Max asked.

"It wasn't me, it was the guy working before me. I'd never let a customer get that far," Luc said.

"How long have you been on the island?" Max asked.

"I came here for a two-week vacation three years ago and I never left," Luc replied.

"You don't miss your old life?" Max asked, suddenly interested.

Luc only shrugged and said, "I love it here. I'm saving up to open my own bar. I'm starting with one, anyway."

Max was impressed. Luc was living, literally, in paradise and still had plans. "You're ambitious. I like that. Anyway, watch out for guys like this when you do open."

Just then, Stan shifted and slipped from their grasp, sliding to the floor with a thud. A few minutes later, they carried him into his suite. As they brought him into the bedroom, Stan's loose hand slid over a table, knocking over some junk food, a few wrappers, and the carry case for the diamond. They had to step around it to drop Stan on the bed.

Lloyd was snoring as soon as he hit the mattress. His job done, Max turned to go and then stopped for a second. Turning back around, he pulled the blanket over Stan's unconscious body.

"Tell anyone I tucked him in, I'll kill you," Max said.

"Sure, Mr. Burdett," Luc said.

Max smiled at the bartender, put his hand on Luc's

shoulder as they headed for the door, and said, "And call me Max."

Max dropped Luc off back at the bar and then drove on. He found the right spot, pulled off the road, and navigated a dirt path down toward an isolated beach. He found the cove quickly, orienting himself according to the rickety old pier that snaked out into the water.

Following a line from the pier, he walked through the scrub to locate the tarp he'd left behind. He was pleased to see that it looked undisturbed. He'd chosen the spot carefully and hidden his equipment well. Pulling back the tarp, Max revealed the trailer tied to a tree with a padlock. On the trailer was the six-foot rubber raft, a Zodiac, filled with scuba equipment.

That was it. Everything was in place and the time was drawing near. Max felt the old rush of excitement and felt it fully for the first time since Napoleon II: he was on a job, and it felt great.

Of course there was still Lola to deal with. Well, he would just have to handle her until it was all over. She'd been patient; all he needed was a little bit more of the same from her.

Max headed back home. The house was dark, which was unusual this time of night. And the door was closed . . . something neither of them did when the other was out. Max reached for the handle and was surprised to see that it was locked. Lola must have locked it by mistake.

"Forgot we even had locks," he said to himself. He

certainly didn't have a key. "Lola!" he called out, but no one answered.

Reaching into his pocket, Max pulled out the small pry bar and tension tools he always kept with him. He began picking the lock. Before he could finish, he heard Lola's voice from inside. "It's locked. And don't try to break in. You're not welcome," she said. Her voice was restrained anger, a tone between fury and ice that he had only heard her use a few times.

"I finished the deck. And you promised to spend the first sunset on it together."

"Lola," Max began, but Lola cut him off.

"That's not all—I found your notebook."

This had gone far enough. "Lola. I'll sit down right now and write the vows—" he began.

Lola cracked the door so that he could barely make out her face. "The vows are not for me. They're for you. You have to figure out if what we have means anything to you. The only thing you've ever been able to commit to is taking other people's possessions. But do you have any of your own?"

Max listened and tried to think of something to say, something to make her open the door, something to make things right between them.

"Max, I'm right here. But I'm not gonna wait much longer," she said.

"Lola, when I watch you sleep, or work around the house, even play tennis, I ask myself, 'What kind of a man could put this at risk?'"

Max tried to put the rest of it into words, in a way that would make her understand and not put her at any further risk. But apparently, Lola was not in a patient mood—whatever she needed to hear, that wasn't it. Lola shut the door.

"Where am I supposed to go?" he said.

He prided himself on his ability to plan jobs down to the smallest detail, and to allow for every possible contingency. Up until now, his success rate had been nearly one hundred percent.

But Max hadn't seen this coming. He hadn't planned for it, hadn't even considered it a possibility. For a moment, he didn't know what to do next. Then he realized he had to do what he'd do if he was on a job: improvise.

Chapter Eleven

Almost two hours later, Max banged on the door, loudly. Then he banged again. Finally, after a delay, a bleary-eyed Stan opened it. From the look on his face, Max could tell that Stan had moved on from dead drunk to spectacularly hungover.

"She threw me out," Max said.

Stan shrugged. "The wages of sin. Why's it my problem?"

"Because every hotel room in the island is booked," Max said, pushing his way in the door. Staying with Stan was his least favorite option, but there were no other rooms available—and Max was technically paying for the suite anyway.

Inside the bedroom, Stan collapsed back into the bed and Max realized that Agent Lloyd would have given him more trouble if he hadn't been so . . . *incapacitated*.

Max took off his jeans, shoes, and socks and eyed the couch. It was full of Lloyd's electronic listening devices. Scanning the equipment, Max saw that it was all new and state-of-the-art. The FBI must want him pretty bad to run an operation like this outside of the United States.

Of course, right now the thousands of dollars of equipment was the only thing between him and even a bad night's sleep. "Can I move the surveillance stuff?" Max asked.

"Don't mess with it, it's expensive," Stan said. It was true, the equipment probably represented a year's worth of Stan's salary.

"I'm not sleeping on the floor," Max said.

"Then you're out of luck."

Well, Max wasn't going to be the only one to suffer. He moved to the bed. "We both are. Move over," he said.

Groaning, Stan moved over. Max lay down next to him on the bed, pulling the blanket over them.

"So what'd you do?" Stan asked.

"I missed our first sunset on her new deck," Max replied.

"That's it?" Stan replied. Max understood—when he put it that way, it didn't sound like much, but it was only part of the reason.

"I've missed them all since we got here. I'm no good at sunsets," he said.

"Of course you're not," Stan said. Then he looked over at Max and continued, "The world's divided up between people who like to watch the sun set and those who don't. I'll bet you wake up with the sun and don't even notice it up there, right?" Max nodded, it was true. For a moment, he was uncomfortable, as if Stan knew him better than someone in the FBI should.

"Exactly," Stan continued. "People like you are never happy. They're anxious, type A, egocentric perfectionists who can't sit still, and die alone with a thousand regrets. But people who can relax and enjoy the sunset, holding hands at the end of the day, they're the happy ones."

Then Max realized where Stan's insight came from. "So why can't you do it?" Max asked.

"Because of you," Stan said, but Max realized that it was only part of the answer. Certainly, Max had set Stan back, but the rest of the reason was because they were alike, much more alike than Max would have thought before and more than he would like to admit even now.

Stan pulled the cover up and said, "Don't hog the blanket."

Sophie arrived at the Atlantis in the morning, heading straight for the Bridge Suite. The hotel manager was already waiting with her ex-husband, Zacharias, as well as the two men he had told her about. These new two were very clean-cut and stood like they had been impaled on steel spikes. Though she hadn't met them yet, she knew the type.

"What'd you drag me down here for?" she asked of the taller one.

"You'll see. Crack it open," he said. His face and voice was unreadable. Something strange was going on, but she'd be damned if she knew what it was. Inside, they headed for the bedroom, and Sophie saw what was without a doubt the single most surprising sight of her law enforcement career: Stanley Lloyd and Max Burdett in bed together.

She blinked, not trusting her eyes. It was, after all, impossible, and on more than one level. The taller man looked down at the scene and said, "The Bureau's got a 'Don't Ask, Don't Tell,' policy, but this is pushing it, Stan," he said.

"Kowalski. Stafford," Stan said. So he knew them, Sophie realized. It made sense now, sort of.

The shorter one, the one called Stafford, pointed to Zacharias and said, "We got a call from Captain Bethel . . . He wanted to know the scope of the FBI's operation on the island. Since we don't have an operation on the island, we came here to check it out."

That was it. Stan was on his own. Suddenly a lot of pieces fell into place and a dozen different doubts were answered. Looking at Max's face, Sophie realized that she wasn't the only one who was surprised here. "What's he talking about, Stan?"

"Let me explain—" he said, to her and to the other agents.

Zacharias answered her question, though, "He's on suspension. Has been for three months."

"Suspension?" Max asked.

"He was deemed unstable after he lost Napoleon II," Agent Kowalski said.

"I guess all he needed was to curl up with a strong, handsome man," Stafford said.

"You told me you were here on the case," was all she could say to Stan.

"I am on the case. I'm gonna catch him, get reinstated, upped, and these slobs'll be saluting me."

For a moment Sophie wondered if Stan really *was* unstable. What he was hoping for was unlikely, to say the least. But even if she accepted that he had his reasons and he meant what he said, that did not begin to explain why he was in bed with the man he had been trying to put away for the last seven years.

Agents Kowalski and Stafford traded a look and Kowalski said, "You've lost your objectivity. Your feelings for Burdett have gone from obsession to identification."

"I'm plenty objective," he said with complete confidence, though Sophie thought the statement was undermined by the fact that both he and Max were still under the covers together.

"Really?" Agent Stafford said.

Max sat up straight and spoke for the first time since they had arrived. "Look, guys, you've got this wrong. Agent Lloyd has done nothing but harass me since the minute he got here. He's the model G-man."

"And he's nothing but a suspect to me," Stan said.

At that, Agent Stafford pulled out surveillance photos of Stan and Max on their fishing trip. There were photos of them talking like old friends and then shots of them putting suntan lotion on each other's back. Up until now, Sophie was hoping that there was an explanation for why Max and Stan were in bed together, other than the obvious. Now she was thinking that it might be best not to overlook the obvious.

"That's not what these show. You guys look plenty chummy," Agent Kowalski said.

"Your 'suspect's' even paying for this suite," Agent Stafford added.

"And the seaweed body wrap," Kowalski said.

Finally, Agent Stafford asked the question that was on everybody's mind: "Are you guys dating?"

Sophie had had it. "You got your slice of paradise. I hope it was everything you thought it would be."

"Sophie—" Stan began, but she didn't intend to stick around for pathetic denials in the face of overwhelming evidence. Before she reached the door, Zacharias took his parting shot. "You might want to do more of a background check before you partner up next time," he said.

With her peripheral vision, Sophie saw Stan jump out of the bed to follow her. She waved him off and hurried for the door.

After the other agents left, Max and Stan did the only thing they could think of: they ordered breakfast. As they waited on the balcony, Max realized that these new developments explained a lot for him. In retrospect, there were a lot of suspicious things going on with respect to Stan's operation on the island. First of all, it was very unusual for an FBI agent to operate outside of the United States, unless he was running an antiterrorism operation. The fact was that foreign powers were even more skittish about having U.S. federal agents roaming around than local American law enforcement was.

Of course, Max had thought that it was a sign of how badly the FBI wanted him, but now he saw that that was his pride talking. He berated himself for letting that happen. Then there was also the question of why Stan was working without a partner. There Max had simply been blinded by the fact that Stan was an FBI agent. As someone who made his living outside the law, it did not even occur to him that a federal officer would do the same.

Shaking his head, Max realized that he was slipping. Maybe retirement had affected him and maybe it *was* time for him to exit the game. *No, it's not time,* a voice in his head said, *at least not yet.* Just one more job.

Of course the jails and the morgues were full of guys who had wanted to pull *just one more job.* The fact was, everyone who was caught was caught on their last job—that's what made it their last job. And every one of those thieves had one thing in common: they'd done exactly one job too many.

Max knew that he wasn't the only one in trouble here. There were about a dozen things he wanted to say to Stan, but most of them he couldn't say without compromising himself, so he picked the easiest—the one place where he knew exactly how Stan felt. "She didn't have to be so hard on you, storm out like that," he said.

"She's got grounds. The thing you gotta understand about us law enforcement types is: we don't appreciate lying," Stan said.

"Lie. Such an ugly word. Come on, Stan. You fibbed, maybe withheld a little. But lie? Nah. You are an FBI agent working a case . . ."

From his face, Max could see that Stan appreciated the support. "The way you put it doesn't make it sound so bad."

"*I* could explain it to her," Max offered.

Stan took that in and said, "What about you? You're a hell of a catch. And I've seen the way you are with Lola. You love that girl. So you're working out some personal issues. Jousting with some demons. All you need is a little support."

"Exactly," Max agreed.

"Hell, *I* could make her understand," Stan said.

Max looked Stan in the eye and saw that they had an agreement. "I'll set it up with Sophie. I don't think she wants to hear from you," Max said.

"And I'll call Lola," Stan said.

"Done," Max said.

They made the calls and set up meetings for that night. Then Max went shopping, picking up some clothes and the few things he'd need until then. Then he went back to the room to wait. Stan was doing the same. Both men watched the clock until it was time and headed out to the small seaside cove they'd agreed upon.

"You think Sophie'll show?" Stan said.

"I did my best," Max said. It was true. He'd tried to be convincing but she was on guard and virtually accused him of cooking this up with Stan. Of course, she was right.

"I did the same, but I can't guarantee anything," Stan said.

Max shrugged and looked out over the water.

"It's the ship's last night. By tomorrow that diamond will be heading back to Paris, and you'll never see it again," Stan said.

"Then it'll be over," Max said. It was true. One way or another, it was true.

Stan was seated at a small candlelit table set up on a beach, adorned with flowers and a bottle of wine, staring intently at Lola, who was seated across from him. "Max can't eat, can't sleep. He's like an injured bird."

At that moment, Max was also seated at a table, staring intently at his own dinner companion, Sophie. He leaned forward earnestly as he said, "Stan's hurt. He's in pain. He's like a wounded dog."

"He needs you Lola," Stan was saying, "you're his better half. Just give him one more chance."

Max was working on a similar tack with Sophie. "He's a good guy," he told her. "Sure, he's a liar—but that comes with the job."

Sophie leaned back in her chair, and slowly shook her head. "I don't know. This is all a bit strange. What do you think, Lola?"

Lola was incredulous. *Couldn't these guys have played this a little smoother,* she thought. *Couldn't they at least have arranged to hold these little heart-to-hearts at different tables, let alone different locations?* "I'm not buying a word of it," Lola said.

"I'm with you," Sophie replied. The two women began to rise, but Max and Stan leapt to their feet to stop them.

"Just hear us out," Max said. "Look, tonight the lies stop."

Sophie and Lola halted, curious now at what Max had to say.

"He's serious," said Stan. "It's over. He's not chasing it, and I'm not chasing it."

"Sorry, I can't believe you until that ship is gone," Lola said.

"And we've still got a few hours before she sails," Sophie added.

"I can't make that ship disappear tonight," Max said. "But I can make us disappear."

"What are you talking about?" said Lola.

"I found a hobby . . ." With that, Max stepped away from the table and lifted up an old fishing tarp that was strewn inconspicuously on the sand. Beneath the tarp was a pile of scuba gear.

Lola smiled. She felt her resolve buckling. She never could stay angry at Max for long, and she found it especially difficult now when he looked so earnest and vulnerable. "They're cute when they beg," she said.

Max obviously had planned this moment meticulously, like he would plan a job. Another woman might have been insulted, but Lola couldn't help but be pleased. In fact, it was the single most romantic thing Max had done for her in their time together.

"There's an old wreck a few miles off the coast, a Spanish galleon that was taken over by pirates in 1758. It's one of the greatest shallow-water dives in the Caribbean. Let's go," Max said. To the others, Lola knew, Max must have sounded sure of himself. She, however, saw the hope and the need in his voice and could not say no.

They got into the scuba gear quickly. Lola was already something of an expert, but she was impressed by how comfortable Max was with the equipment. He must have been planning this for some time, she realized.

When they were suited up, they got onto the boat and launched. Max sat in the back to start the engine and directed them out to sea. The night was quiet, the sea beautiful. An evening dive had been a great idea. And the fact was that the ship would be gone tomorrow. Max was showing her that he intended to stay honest.

After a few minutes, Max cut the engine and dropped anchor. "All set. Down we go . . ." Max said. Without hesitation, he rolled back into the water with a splash. The others followed.

Lola went next and was struck once again by the warmth of the Caribbean water. During her lessons and dives, she had enjoyed the sense of peace she'd felt, and she remembered thinking *if only Max could get a taste of this*. Well, he seemed to have embraced it. As it was, he'd taken a number of important steps today. And once the diamond was out of reach, it would get easier for him to adjust to their new life.

The others joined them underwater and they dove as

a group toward the ocean floor. They followed Max, who seemed to know exactly where he was going and led them to what looked like a ghostly ruin emerging out of the shadows. Lola followed his flashlight and kept a tight grip on her own.

When they swam closer, the ruin started to look like what it was: a Spanish galleon. It was magnificent. There was a large piece that must have been the center of the ship, and had the remains of a tall mast lying nearby. Then there were perhaps half a dozen other sections that had been separated from the rest of the ship and were spread out over a large area—perhaps a quarter-mile square.

The ship looked like it belonged in a storybook, like it existed in a completely separate world from the world of the surface and the island. The nighttime dive made the illusion even more effective. Well, Max never did anything halfway, she thought, smiling to herself.

"It's beautiful," Lola said, speaking clearly into the microphone so the others could hear her.

"You outdid yourself, Max," Stan said, his voice coming through over the radio.

"Let's check it out," Max's voice said. He swam toward the eerie shipwreck. Lola had to work to keep Max and the others in her sight. She could see their figures only if they were within maybe twenty feet. And even then, it was difficult to tell them apart, and impossible to make out faces.

They reached the wreck and Lola immediately sought out the central section and the mast. After only a few seconds, she realized she couldn't see any of the others and said, "Where are you guys?"

"Watching the lobsters on the deck," came Sophie's reply.

"Checking out the main cabin," Stan said.

"I'm at the back of the wreck," Max said. Lola looked in that direction and could just make out his swimming form.

"That would be the stern, Max," Lola said, smiling to herself. Max still had a few things to learn, but there would be plenty of time for that now. And she thought they would enjoy doing more of this kind of exploration together.

Lola swam on to explore some more. "Look how far this is spread out," Max said, amazement in his voice. Lola found that she knew exactly how he felt.

Dressed all in black and wearing a mask, the thief looked more like a shadow than a man as he moved forward across the deck of the ship. Though this part of the operation required the least specialized skill, it was the most dangerous. It was still before midnight and there were too many people milling about the ship. Even after taking every possible precaution, there was still a chance of being spotted.

Ironically, the mask that protected his identity would reveal him instantly as a thief to a passenger or a member of the crew. And with all the publicity about the ship's last night near Paradise Island, anything suspicious would be reported immediately. Well, there was always an element of risk in this sort of operation. No one ever won a prize worth tens of millions without taking some chances.

So the thief kept to the shadows and made his way to a service stairway. Most of the crew was off duty, so service areas were safer than public places. Finally, he reached the door and slowly stepped inside the stairwell. There was no one around and no sounds. Smiling to himself, he walked down two decks to the climate control room. As his information showed, it was unmanned. He slipped inside and made his way toward the small access panel. Reaching to his belt with one gloved hand, he pulled out a battery-operated Phillips-head screwdriver.

He immediately went to work on the four screws, and less than two minutes after entering the room, he was inside the air vent. Reaching behind him, he pulled the cover into place. Though he could have taken the time to secure the cover better, he didn't bother. He would be off the ship long before the next shift came on duty.

Quickly, the thief made his way through air vent system. There wasn't much space, but he had never suffered from claustrophobia—a debilitating condition for someone doing this sort of work. In the dim light of the vent system, he made one turn after another. He was glad he had taken the time to memorize the layout of the vents and his path through them. Reading maps was time-consuming and would require light that could potentially give him away.

Checking his watch, he saw that it was time for the midnight shift to come on in the gem exhibit room and the security control room. He'd been watching the ship carefully and knew that the man watching the diamond was, in fact, a retired cop with arthritis. Or, in other words: the thief's dream security guard.

The thief came to a stop above the grate that led to the storage room below. Checking his watch, he confirmed that it was time. Quietly and carefully, he took off the grate and saw the security camera attached to the ceiling in the room below him. Then he pulled out his battery-operated screwdriver and opened an access panel near him in the vent.

With the panel removed, there was a mess of wires exposed to him. Again, his memory did not fail him and he sought out the red wires. Once he found them, he cut them quickly with his wire cutters.

That was it—the feed to the camera was now off and he could move on to the next phase of the plan. Without hesitating, he dropped straight through the grate, landing gracefully and, he thought, quietly on the floor of the storage room.

Reaching into his pack, he pulled out the shape-charge explosives he had prepared. He was no explosive expert himself, but he had had no trouble hiring someone to prepare this charge for him. And he was more than qualified to place the charge and detonate it. Moving swiftly and confidently, he put the charge into place.

This was going to be almost too easy.

In the surveillance room, the guard had just put his coffee down when he saw the impossible on one of the monitors in front of him. In fact, for a full two seconds, he was sure he was looking at a joke, or a drill in progress. Then his mind registered that it was really happening: a masked man dressed in black was placing what looked like explosives against a wall—and doing it in full view of the security camera. He checked the monitor to make sure he was looking at the storage room near the gem exhibit and he saw that he was correct.

"What the hell is that?" he said, pointing to the monitor.

The chief took a look over his shoulder and immediately hit a button on the security panel in front of them. "Intruder in storage facility B! Repeat, intruder, storage facility B! All security to storage facility B. Attempted break-in in progress."

Then the chief was racing for the door and the guard sprinted behind him.

Chapter Twelve

The thief had the charges in place and reached for the detonator. With luck, he would be off the ship less than fifteen minutes from now. After attaching the wires to the detonator, he stuck the other ends of the wires directly into the shape-charges he'd placed on the wall.

And then something happened that wasn't part of the plan: the door to the storage room swung open. Before he could move or even think about escape, half a dozen uniformed security guards swarmed him. The next thing he knew, he was being thrown to the ground.

He thought wildly about escaping. The door was being covered, but if he could get back into the vent . . .

The only problem was the six full-grown men who were now on top of him. He struggled anyway for a few seconds and then it sunk in: he was caught and there was no way out. He felt a hand on his face through the mask; then the mask was off him and six faces were staring into his own.

Jean-Paul knew he was in trouble, but he found that he wasn't thinking of the unpleasant future that lay in front of him. Instead, he had only one thought, one word, running through his mind.

Burdett . . .

Max made his way through the last few yards of the vent. He didn't particularly like being in such a small space, but he'd make do. After all, the reward in this case was certainly worth it. When he reached the grate, he removed it carefully and slid it aside. Suddenly he had an unobstructed view of the Napoleon diamond, less than ten feet below him. *The third one, the last one,* he thought.

Reaching up with one hand, he pulled his mask off—he wouldn't need it now. Then he put on his thermal goggles, night vision equipment optimized to show him the crisscrossing lights of the motion sensors protecting the diamond below. The sensors showed blue through the goggles and Max could see each beam clearly.

So far, the job had gone exactly according to plan. Jean-Paul had played his part perfectly—if not willingly. Now the authorities thought they had the thief in custody and Max had Special Agent Lloyd as his alibi. Max forced himself to keep focused on the task at hand. Over-confidence had put many of his colleagues in prison. And Max knew he wasn't infallible—Stan's bullet had proved that to him.

As if on cue, Stan's voice came through his headset. "Max . . ." he said; then there was static.

Max pressed a button on his remote control and said into the microphone, "What's up?"

"This is really amazing," Stan's voice said.

Hitting the button again, Max said, "Did you see the manta rays?"

"No," Stan replied.

"Keep looking. You'll see them," Max said. He smiled at the genuine enthusiasm in Stan's voice.

Max reached into his backpack and brought out his foot-long cutoff fishing rod he had made to fish on his dock. He positioned it over the Napoleon display and lowered the wire using his makeshift reel and line. Glad for the practice he had gotten fishing, Max was pleased that even his left hand was perfectly steady. He guided the wire precisely between the crisscrossing blue motion sensor beams.

"You . . . *bzzzt* . . . found any buried treasure?" Stan asked.

"Not yet. But I'm still trying," Max replied, looking down at the diamond and smiling.

He brought the wire to a stop just above the unbreakable glass display. Then with one hand he took out an eyedropper and dripped a concentrated hydrofluoric acid down the line. Then he switched eyedroppers and added a few drops of sodium hydroxide. The sodium hydroxide trickled down the wire and landed on the glass, meeting the hydroflouric acid with a sizzle. The combined acid melted the glass, creating a small hole at the top of the display.

Max was pleased that his calculations were correct. Any less and he would not have breached the glass. Any more and he might have damaged the diamond. Seeing that the hole was exactly the right size, Max brought up the line and attached the metal claw to the end and lowered it back down to the case.

Carefully, he placed it right over the diamond and clicked his remote control. The claw opened up. Lowering it further, he hit another button and the claw grasped the diamond securely. Cranking the reel, Max pulled the diamond off its cushion and raised it up towards the vent.

The security chief watched on the storage room monitor as one of the midnight shift security guards pulled the suspect to his feet. He was so battered that he could barely stand. *Well, that should teach him to try to mess with this boat,* the chief thought.

Speaking into his walkie-talkie, the guard on the monitor said, "Suspect is down. Repeat, suspect is down. Storage facility is secure."

Hitting a button on the security console, the chief said, "Lock him up until the local cops get here. And keep at least two guards on him at all times."

The guards probably weren't necessary. Catching this clown had been almost too easy. There was some evidence that he had tried to cut power to the security camera, but he failed for some reason. *Amateur,* the chief thought. It was sort of disappointing in a way. The chief had been expecting Burdett. Now *that* would have been a catch . . .

He would have enjoyed taking that man into custody himself. That would have showed the local PD and the FBI a thing or two. Well, the chief would have to be satisfied with this guy—whoever he was. He didn't carry any ID and wasn't talking. Well, that would change soon enough.

The chief checked the monitor again. The thief was standing there looking lost as guards retrieved the explosives beside him. Turning to the men in the room behind him, the chief said, "Who did he think he was? The Invisible Man?" The men laughed and the chief joined them. It felt damn good.

Next to him, a junior officer's eyes went wide and he grabbed the chief by the arm as he pointed to the monitor. Spinning around, the chief saw something he would not have believed unless he saw it with his own eyes. Seemingly by itself, the diamond was floating up out of its display case and toward the ceiling.

He watched in stunned silence for a few seconds, then saw the line that was pulling the diamond. Once he realized what was going on, he said, "Shit!" He immediately went into action. He hit a switch on the control panel and shouted, "It was a diversion! Get back to the diamond! Get back to the diamond!" Then he hit the general alarm button, and his men flooded out of the room.

Max heard the alarm. It was earlier than he had planned—the guards must have been sharper than he'd anticipated, or someone had gotten lucky. Still, it wasn't a critical problem, at least not yet. Quickly but calmly, he wound up the line and brought the diamond into the vent with him.

Almost on their own, his gloved hands secured the diamond in the pouch on his shoulder and tossed the rod and reel into the backpack. He maintained his cool the whole time, working quickly. When all of the tasks were completed, he performed the final item on his checklist . . .

. . . he hauled ass backward through the vent.

Immediately, he heard the ring of gunshots as they pierced the vent in front of him. Four . . . five . . . then too many to count. Max felt an involuntary twitch in his shoulder but kept moving. As he did, he heard the voice of a panicked guard scream, "We're too late! He's got the diamond! Repeat, he's got the diamond! He's in the vents!"

Scrambling now, Max moved even faster, taking a quick inventory of his body. None of the bullets had hit him. Of course, there was still plenty of time for things to go wrong. And though the vent system ran throughout the ship, movement within it was painfully slow. Pouring it on, he added a little more speed to his awkward, backward crawl. He couldn't even turn around in the confined space of the vent.

Then the vent beneath him groaned and he was

falling. Before he hit the ground, he realized that he must have fallen through a grate . . .

. . . and onto the hard tile floor of a bathroom. No, not just a bathroom, the men's room off of the ballroom. It was where he meant to go, even if he'd planned for a more dignified entrance.

"Oof!" he said as he hit the ground, realizing that he hit the remote for his headset as he fell.

Lola heard Max make a sound, as if he hit something, or ran into something. It sounded like a crash and an "Oof!" Faint, but she recognized it immediately. There was something wrong with the sound, like it wasn't the kind you ever made underwater. Immediately suspicious, she said, "Is that you, Max, way over on the stern?"

In the distance, she could barely make out a diver swimming near the stern. He was a long way off from the other parts of the boat.

"I'm floating around," Max said, his voice calm, too calm for Lola's liking.

"I'm heading starboard. Come see me when you're done," she said.

"Sure," Max replied.

Without hesitating, Lola swam straight toward the diver at the stern, who was facing away from her now. He seemed to be studying the boat. Over the radio, Max said, "There's musket holes in the wood here. The boat must have taken a battering."

Okay, that had to be Max, she thought . . . *except it*

wasn't. Something was wrong with the way he carried himself, the way he moved in the water. Swimming faster, she reached for the diver, grabbed him by the shoulder and turned him around.

It was Luc, the bartender from the tiki bar. He smiled sheepishly at her, looking embarrassed.

"Who knows what else we'll find down here," Max's voice said over the radio.

"Isn't that the truth," Lola replied.

In the bathroom, Max got to his feet. As he did, he heard the door open around the corner. Someone was coming, several someones by the sound of it. That was it. He was caught. He was going to stand out like . . . well, like a thief in a wet suit.

As soon as he heard their voices, he realized they were passengers. "What's the alarm for?" one asked.

"Not enough champagne, emergency," a second replied.

"Too many straight men, emergency," a third voice added. Laughing, the three men stepped in front of Max. The took one look at him in his wet suit, and didn't bat an eye.

"Hi," one of them said.

And then Max realized why they weren't surprised to see him dressed like he was. All of them were wearing costumes: one was a sailor, one was a deep-sea diver, one a submarine commander, and the last one Aquaman.

The deep-sea diver looked him over and said, "Great costume."

Smiling, Max said, "Thanks." Then he headed for the door and the hallway beyond. Outside the men's room, he saw a banner that read WELCOME TO KING NEPTUNE'S UNDERSEA BALL!

Partygoers were moving down the corridor toward the ballroom, all of them dressed in some kind of underwater costume. Security guards started swarming the hallway, looking for him. One of the guards turned to another two and said, "Everyone stay calm. Please return to your cabins immediately."

Max joined a group of mermaids and sailors as they moved through the exit. Squeezing past the guards, Max bumped into one. As he did he heard Stan's voice over the radio say, "I'm heading for the stern."

Lola stared at Luc, wondering what they hell she was supposed to do now. She could see that Luc was nervous and didn't know what to do himself. If he stayed where he was, Stan would figure out what was going on. If he swam away, it would look too suspicious . . . *and* Stan would figure out what was going on. He looked at her desperately. Lola just shook her head. This was not her problem. Max had done this to himself.

"I'll be there in a second. I want to see those musket holes," Stan said.

On the sky deck, Max made his way past the rock-climbing wall and volleyball courts. The ship was full of people moving in all directions, making their way to their cabins. Whatever he did, he had to do it quickly. In a few minutes the deck would be empty and he would be alone and out in the open.

"There you are. I can see you," Stan's voice said over the speaker. Max froze, the jig was up. He cursed himself for his pride. This was never a one-person job. He was good, one of the two best thieves in the world, but there were too many variables to handle it all by himself.

He had told himself that he'd done it all for Lola, to protect her, to keep her out of trouble, to let her have the life she wanted. Well, she'd have that life now, but it wouldn't be with him.

Lola wanted to strangle Max, but she'd never get the chance if his cover was blown, and Stan was swimming toward them right now, less than fifteen feet away. She realized that a piece of the wreckage was blocking her from his view.

Ten feet . . .

Eight . . .

"Be with you in one second," Stan said.

He was just about to reach Luc when Lola made her move. She swam out through a hold in the wreck and glided silently behind Stan, quickly reaching out and turning a valve at the top of his tank. Then she pulled back.

Immediately, a rush of bubbles escaped from his rig. Stan came to a quick stop and said, "I've got an air problem!"

Swimming back next to Stan, Lola said, "It's okay. I'm right here." Uncoiling her spare respirator, she handed it toward him. "Here. Take my octopus."

"You okay, Stan?" Sophie's voice came over the radio. Lola could hear her concern.

"He'll be fine. I've got him," Lola said.

"Guide me up," Stan said, sounding concerned but not panicked. He had to take off his mask to breathe from the spare respirator—meaning that, for the moment, he could not see. With her peripheral vision, Lola saw that Luc was taking the opportunity to move to a safer part of the wreck.

"You guys okay?" Max's voice said.

"I can come up," Sophie offered.

Lola guided Stan up to the surface. "We'll be fine. I'll reset his valve, we'll be right back."

That was all she could do—buy Max a few minutes. He had to be close by, to be in radio range. Of course, Lola had a very good idea exactly where Max was at the moment.

"He was lucky I was there to save his ass," Lola said, and Max had no doubt at all who she was speaking to.

Max breathed a sigh of relief as he moved into a crowd. As soon as she heard Stan say he was having trouble with his air, he suspected Lola was involved somehow. The timing was impeccable and exactly her style.

* * *

The security chief had to see the gem room for himself. Standing in front of the empty display case he could only shake his head. "How did this happen?" he said to the guards around him. Truly, it made no sense.

His security was cutting-edge, state-of-the-art. And even so, it didn't rely completely on expensive toys. There were human operators and people watching every monitor at all times. All of that effort, and he'd been beaten by a diversion, an almost childishly simple act of misdirection.

The thief—Burdett, he was sure—had used an accomplice to keep all of their attention in the storage room while he made off with the goods. Well, it wasn't over yet. He still had a suspect in custody and there was a chance that Burdett was still on board—and if he was they would find him.

Leaving the exhibit room, the chief headed for the storeroom that was serving as their makeshift brig and interrogation room. He had to move quickly; once the local PD took charge of the suspect the chief would be out of the loop. There were only minutes now for him to redeem himself and get the damned diamond back.

One of the midnight-shift guards had the battered suspect up against the wall. So far they'd learned that his name was Jean-Paul and he was a known accomplice of Henry Moore. That was an interesting wrinkle—one they had precious little time to fully sort out. When the chief approached, Jean-Paul looked up at him, still too stunned to believe that he had been captured.

"How did you see me? I did everything right," he said.

"You forgot to cut the camera feed, genius," the guard said.

"I did. I cut the red wires," Jean-Paul protested.

"You cut the red wires?" the guard asked and Jean-Paul nodded. "Congratulations. You cut the heating to the Jacuzzi."

The chief had seen enough. He grabbed the suspect by the neck and pushed him, hard up against the wall. "Your partner got away. Who was he?"

"I don't have a partner," Jean-Paul said.

Pieces started to fit together in the chief's mind. Thing's were making sense, though that didn't mean their chances of recovering the diamond were getting any better. Then the guard next to him said what the chief was thinking: "What were you then, the moronic decoy?"

On the main deck, Max watched the security guards search. They checked behind every table, every chair, and opened every door. Good. They were searching the ship for him and weren't anticipating his next move. To be fair, ship's security was on board mostly to settle disputes between passengers, break up the occasional fight, and deal with petty theft. Max played his game at an entirely different level.

He made his way to the railing and saw that his rappelling line was in place. Making sure that the guards were looking elsewhere, he attached his harness to the line and flipped over the railing. He made his way down the rope carefully. There was no point in hurrying. If he'd already been seen, he wouldn't be able to get away fast enough, and a fall from this height to the water would be no picnic.

Looking down, he could see his second Zodiac waiting for him. He was mildly surprised to see the boat. It should have been the first thing the guards spotted after the alarm was sounded. Obviously, they were stuck on the idea of catching him on board the ship, so much so that they didn't bother to think about possible escape routes. He could have swum back to the wreckage, but it would have taken time and made it more likely that Stan would figure out what was going on.

Finally, he reached his boat and settled into it just as he heard Lola say, "All clear. Must've gotten jammed."

"You guys coming back down?" Max said into the headset.

"We're on the way," Stan said.

Max cut the line to his anchor and sped away on the Zodiac as the alarms on the cruise ship blared behind him. Looking back, he saw that no one was tracking him, and he continued to shore. When he reached land, he moved quickly to conceal the boat behind the reef. Then he allowed himself a moment to reach into his shoulder pocket and pull out the diamond. It was amazing, like the first two had been.

Nevertheless, Max found that the exhilaration he usually felt at the end of a job was eluding him. There was no satisfaction, no feeling of accomplishment. Then he realized why. This job wasn't finished, not by a long shot. Getting the diamond was only the first phase of this operation. The most difficult part still lay ahead of him: he had to face Lola.

After securing the diamond again, he dove into the water and swam toward where the other Zodiac was anchored and his friends were diving.

Chapter Thirteen

Max swam down to the ocean floor, the Spanish galleon wreckage in front of him. He noticed a lobster crawling near the ship. He made sure he was clear and swam toward the rocks behind the wreck. He went the long way around so none of the others would see him and finally reached the area behind the rocks where Luc was huddled, waiting for him.

The bartender gave him a thumbs-up, which Max returned, but he saw that Luc was a bit shaken. Well, not everyone was cut out for this kind of work, and Luc *was* an excellent bartender. In fact, his pay for this night's work would go a long way toward making his dream of owning his own bar a reality.

As Luc swam away, Max spoke into the radio, "My tank's getting low. Ready to surface?" The others all said yes and Max added, "Let's meet up by the keel, go up together."

About two minutes later, Max reached the keel at the same time as the other three. There were nods all around and they surfaced, taking care not to rise faster than their bubbles—a simple safety measure that helped divers avoid the bends. Max noted that Lola wouldn't even look in his direction as they ascended. This part of the operation would be very tough indeed, he realized.

After a few minutes, they reached the Zodiac and climbed on board, everyone taking off their masks and respirators.

"That was amazing," Sophie said, smiling.

Stan was smiling as well. He slapped Max on the back and said, "I'm gonna have to review every bad thing I've ever said about you." Then Stan sat next to Sophie, and Max could see that they were a couple again.

Lola kept her distance and did not smile. Max started the motor and guided the ship to shore. When they reached their isolated cove, Max tied up the boat and everyone took off the rest of their equipment.

"And now, a toast . . ." Max said, reaching for the champagne he had brought on the Zodiac.

"What are we celebrating?" Stan asked.

"Retirement," Max said. After pouring each of them a drink, he held up his glass. Lola didn't react and Max saw that Stan noticed. Still, Stan raised his own glass. "I'll drink to that," Stan said.

All four of them took a drink, and Sophie's cell phone rang. Digging into her purse, she looked at the phone. "Ten messages?" she said to herself as she put the phone to her ear. "Hello . . . What? How?"

Sophie was clearly stunned and Max had a pretty good idea about the news she had just received. "I'll be right there," she said finally.

"What's wrong?" Stan asked, but Max could see that he was already starting to guess.

"The diamond's been stolen," she said.

"What?" Stan asked.

"Ten minutes ago. While we were down there," she said. Suddenly all eyes were on Max. No, not all eyes. Lola wouldn't even look at him. Still, Max did his best to look innocent.

A cold calm washed over Stan. He took a step to Max and said, "You set us up. This whole thing."

"Come on," Max said, sounding indignant.

"You got your perfect alibi: me," Stan said.

Shaking his head, Max said, "I was down there with you and the lobsters the whole time . . ."

Stan just looked at him in mute disbelief.

Suddenly, Sophie was all business. "Get your hands up," she said and then patted Max down. "No wonder you just retired. You've got nothing left to steal."

Finally she reached into his wet suit's shoulder pocket . . . and brought out nothing. As Sophie searched the Zodiac, Max was glad he had taken the extra time to hide the diamond properly.

As she stepped back onto the pier, Stan turned to Max and said, "You couldn't resist, could you? You had to screw me one last time. You had to make an ass out of me." He threw his champagne glass into the water and continued. "Congratulations, friend. You actually had me fooled."

Max had no response for that. Every word Stan had said was true. And while no one would starve to death because of the loss of the diamond, Stan would pay another price here. On the other hand, the only way for Stan to come out on top in this situation would be if he caught Max in the act and put him in prison for a very long time. On balance, Max thought a bit of extra embarrassment for Agent Lloyd was worth it.

Apparently, Stan didn't think so.

Then Lola turned her back to him and walked away. "Lola, wait," Max said, trying to put everything he was thinking and feeling into those words. He knew he was failing miserably and found that he was stuck without a backup plan.

Still, he would have to come up with something. The stakes on this one were everything.

In the holding area, the security chief watched as his guards prepared to haul Jean-Paul off the boat. Captain Bethel and his junior officers stepped forward to take him into custody. This was it, the end of the diamond. Even if it was recovered now because of something the suspect said, the chief was out of the loop. Credit would go to local PD.

The chief had lost and didn't like it one bit. "His partner got away," he said to Bethel, who nodded and answered his ringing cell phone.

"We just got a fiber match from the schematics theft. We know who his partner is," Captain Bethel said. He didn't look happy either.

"Who is it?" the chief asked.

Bethel looked uncomfortable. "I can't say right now, in case it turns out to be nothing," he said.

There was something going on, alright. Whoever it was, there was much more going on here than *nothing*.

Bethel knew that he had to handle this raid himself. It wasn't that it would be sensitive—though there were plenty of local politicians who would be pretty damn *sensitive* tomorrow. It was because he had done so much to help this man, intervened on permits, given free security on construction and other projects. He had also overlooked reports that tied Moore to gambling and other vice-related businesses.

He had been wrong about Henry Moore. And Sophie had been right. It galled him to admit that his ex-wife had caught something so important that he had missed. She was still a little green, but she was a good cop with good instincts. And for all his years of experience, he had been taken in by Moore's progressive talk, and his "What's good for business is good for the people" bullshit.

Most importantly, Bethel had ignored the little voice inside that was telling him all along that something didn't add up. Well, it was time to change that. Moore's right hand, Jean-Paul, was caught red-handed trying to blow his way into the gem exhibit. That had smoothed the way for a few search warrants, and now fibers from Moore's clothing matched fibers taken from the scene of the schematics robbery on board the ship. Moore was a crook, plain and simple, and once Bethel saw that truth, he couldn't unsee it.

Well, Bethel might have lost his investigative edge, but he would be damned if he couldn't still make an arrest in the face of overwhelming evidence. He put together his team quickly, pulling men from the wrap-up on the cruise ship and got everyone moving in less than fifteen minutes. They reached Moore's headquarters five minutes after that.

A dozen officers streamed out of cars, guns drawn. Bethel drew his own weapon and headed for the door. If Moore was playing for stakes as high as the diamond, then there would likely be trouble—especially considering some of the rumors about his *businesses* that up until now Bethel had decided to ignore.

The four officers he assigned to the front door swung the steel battering ram and the door nearly exploded open. The four officers stepped aside and Bethel led the remaining men inside. The old brick building was quiet, as if empty, but Bethel proceeded with caution. He and his men methodically checked each room and confirmed they were all empty.

One of the rumors about Moore's operation at this site was that he was running an after-hours club, one that had illegal gambling and the inevitable prostitutes and drugs that went with it. Bethel had once asked Moore about the rumors, and the man had simply smiled and said that he did run a private after-hours club where friends could meet late at night. Bethel had accepted his answer then. Now he was sure that what had gone on in here was much worse than what he had heard. His instincts might have been asleep before, but they were wide-awake now, and they were screaming that Moore was dangerous. Suddenly, he was very glad he had worn his Kevlar vest and had ordered his men to do the same.

With most of the building checked, there was only one door left to bust through. The boys with the battering ram opened it quickly, and Bethel was the first one through. He thought he was ready for anything, but not for what he found . . .

The large room was completely empty.

Still, the scent of stale, spilled liquor and sweat filled the air. That told him that this had been the place. Moore must have cleared out in a hurry since Jean-Paul had been nabbed. Something told Bethel that Moore had vacated the premises just minutes before they arrived. Still, he could be anywhere now.

It would take time to track down all of Moore's various offices and run the plates for all of his cars. In the meantime, Moore would be out there.

Max and Lola drove home in separate cars. Jumping out, Max immediately went to her side. He said the very first thing he could think to say: "You really did save me down there."

She ignored him, opened the front door, and stepped

inside. Max was mildly surprised that she didn't shut the door in his face. It wasn't much, but, at this point, Max was prepared to take what he could get.

Lola kept walking. Max followed and said, "I'm sorry I kept you in the dark, but I was trying to protect you."

"How generous of you," she said.

"You were right, I couldn't do it without you. But you gotta admit, the look on Stan's face was poetry," he said.

Ignoring him, she opened the bedroom door and stepped inside. Max followed. Lola immediately opened her closet and pulled out a suitcase, tossing it onto the bed. Suddenly, he realized why she had not closed the door in his face. She wasn't going to throw him out; she was going to leave.

After opening the suitcase, she began throwing clothes into it. He grabbed her hand to stop her. "Don't," he said, trying not to sound as defeated as he felt.

"I saved you, Max, because I love you. And now I'm leaving you," she said. Closing the suitcase, she picked it up off the bed. Leaving the bedroom, she headed straight for the front door.

"I thought you'd appreciate how I did it. You of all people . . ." he said, realizing that he was dangerously close to babbling.

"I do, Max. It was a smart plan. You're a great thief. But I want a great man," she said.

That hurt. He realized that he never before bothered to make a distinction between the two. Lola opened the door and headed out, then closed it gently behind her. He saw that that was worse than slamming it—more permanent somehow.

This was impossible. She couldn't leave. It couldn't be over. For a moment, he saw his father giving up on life, sitting in his chair in a quiet house, and Max felt himself teetering on the edge of something dark. Max wasn't sure what he was going to do, but he knew that he had to stop Lola from leaving.

He'd simply have to improvise.

As he opened the door, he said, "Lola . . ." And then Max froze. He was looking at Henry Moore standing next to Lola, his arm around her neck as he held a gun to her temple. Max felt a sick feeling in his stomach. Suddenly he didn't care if she left him. He only wanted to make sure she got out of this alive. After all, he had gotten her into this. He had set up Moore, depending on the police to do the rest. Well, apparently, Moore had managed to stay one step ahead of them.

Now Moore looked . . . desperate. He knew that the police were after him and he'd come for the one thing he could still have before he either escaped the island or was caught: revenge. Okay, two things: revenge *and* the diamond.

"Get inside," Moore said, his voice tightly controlled.

Max stepped back in as Moore pushed him with one hand and Lola with the other. This was very bad. Moore was a wild card that Max hadn't considered. Once again, he had no contingency plan for this situation and none of his many skills would do much good here.

Trapped, a voice in his mind said. *You're both trapped.*

It was true. He didn't see a way out. As for improvisation, he took one look at Lola and felt a cold fear settling into his stomach. At the moment, he was completely out of ideas.

Stan waited at the marina as Sophie talked on the phone. When she hung up, she said, "They raided Moore's headquarters. Nothing." Stan nodded. Sophie gave him a look and said, "But how did he do it?"

"He's a master at alibis," Stan said. "They're his art."

"But he was with us, we went diving together," she said.

Stan remembered the faked video at the basketball game. Everyone saw Max on the screen while he was making off with the diamond. "Did you actually see his face once we were under the surface?" She shook her head. "He had somebody cover for him, used a radio transmitter to talk to us while he was taking the diamond," he said with a shrug. A few things hadn't added up when they were diving the wreck, but Stan hadn't guessed that Max had gone AWOL. He had seriously thought Max had given up on the diamond. Of course, he'd been disappointed, on a number of different levels.

"Do you think Lola knew?" Sophie asked him.

"Did you see the way she was looking at him?" Stan asked.

"Yeah, but I figured she was still mad from before," Sophie said.

"I'm sure she was, but she was *angrier* than before. I think she actually figured it out when we were underwater. Look, I'm still a little fuzzy on some of the details, but I know one thing: Max took the diamond and has it stashed somewhere," Stan said as they walked to Sophie's car.

"What about Jean-Paul? Were they working together?" Lola asked.

"I don't think so, or at least I don't think Jean-Paul knew he was being set up to take Max's fall," Stan said.

"But we suspected that Max might be working with Moore," she said.

"Now I think Max set up both Moore and Jean-Paul. They were supposed to go for the diamond, but Max never meant for them to get it or even a share in it," Stan said.

"Even now, you can't help but respect him," Sophie said, studying him.

Stan nodded. "This was probably his best work." And for Max Burdett, that was saying a lot.

As they got into the car, she said, "You know, I think he was still your friend."

"What?" Stan replied.

"He was just following his nature. Just like you were just following yours when you tried to put him away. You like each other, and I do think he was your friend," Sophie said.

"Well, if he does all this to me when he's my friend, I only hope I never get on his bad side," Stan said roughly. But he thought about what Sophie was saying. There was more than a little truth to it, he knew, but somehow that didn't make him feel one bit better. Stan had gone off the reservation for this one. He was operating in a foreign country and would have no jurisdiction even if he was still on active duty. *And* he was on suspension. As it stood, he was just a private U.S. citizen sticking his nose where it didn't belong and ensuring that he was an even bigger laughingstock back at the FBI.

They thought he was unstable before. He could only imagine what Assistant Director Kirsh would make of this fiasco, and how it would look on his next psych evaluation.

"Men like you and Max can't help being what they are. Even men like Henry Moore can't help being gangsters," Sophie said.

"So we should just let them be?" Stan said.

"Not at all. We should follow our *own* natures and put them away. We just can't win every one. We didn't get anything on Max, but we've got plenty on Moore," she said.

"But he's still free," Stan said.

"True, but not for long," Sophie said.

"Well, I wouldn't want to be Max if Moore gets a hold of him before your department puts him away," Stan said.

"Yeah," Sophie said. Something in that struck Stan. By the look on Sophie's face, he thought that she was thinking the same thing. Even if Moore was trying to get off the island, there was one stop he would want to make before he left.

"Turn around," Stan said. Even as the words were leaving his lips, Sophie was putting the car into a skid and swinging it around. If Moore had already gotten to Max and Lola's, it was already too late. Hurrying now and saving a few seconds wouldn't make a difference.

They hurried anyway.

* * *

As soon as Moore entered the room, he cracked Max hard across the mouth with the butt of his gun. Max went down, hard, and he could immediately feel blood dripping from his mouth.

As Max tried to get his bearings, Moore said, "I tried to deal with you from an elevated place. But I see I have to get down in the gutter. Where's the *motherfucking diamond*?"

Pushing himself up to his hands and knees, Max turned his head to see that Moore had tightened his grip on Lola. Max's eyes met hers, and in that moment he saw the utter stupidity of what he'd done. He could have told her about Moore. They could have solved it together. Hell, even going to Stan for help would have been better than this. But Max's pride had gotten in the way. He wanted to prove that he could beat them all, and get the diamond on his own.

Well, he'd won every game he'd played, but he was about to lose the only one that mattered—and so was Lola, who had no part in this whole mess. He was ready to pay the price for his own hubris, but he couldn't bear the thought of Lola paying the bill for him.

"She had nothing to do with this," Max said.

"She does now," Moore said, the threat clear. Lola was his leverage against Max, his insurance that Max cooperate and give him what he wanted. And Max would do it—he would gladly give up the diamond and anything else to keep her safe. And once he'd given

Moore everything he asked for, Max had no doubt that the gangster would kill them both anyway.

Max found that he was completely out of tricks.

Moore put the gun to Lola's temple, but before he had time to finish the movement, Lola reached up with a sudden movement and knocked it out of his hand, sending it flying across the room. Furious, Moore grabbed her by the hair and tossed her to the floor.

Max leapt from his crouching position and dove for the gun, but Moore was there first. Max turned on the ground to see Moore swing the pistol toward him, but before Moore could complete the action there was a flash of movement. Suddenly, there was a screwdriver sticking out of Moore's thigh.

Both men turned to Lola. Moore gritted his teeth against the pain and said, "Nice . . . throw . . . bitch."

Instead of going down, Moore steeled himself and retrained the gun on Max. "You're taking me back. I haven't shot a man since I was seventeen."

As Moore stared down at him, Max wondered if the man would demand the diamond or if he would shoot first and then search the house for it. Looking into Moore's eyes, Max knew the answer. He steeled himself for the shot that would come any second now. And at this range, it would take only one bullet for each of them.

There was a loud bang . . . no, not a bang, a crash. Something came flying through the shutters in the front of the house—two somethings that rolled to the ground. Before Max could even register that it was Stan and Sophie, Stan was firing his weapon—a single shot that took Moore practically dead center in his chest.

Instantly, Moore crashed to the ground. Max didn't have to check his pulse to see that the gangster was dead.

Max stood up, turned to Moore, and said, "The people have spoken."

Stan and Sophie rushed over to check the body, but Max wasn't going to give that trash another second of his time. He went to Lola and embraced her.

"It's over now. All of it," he said.

Max hugged her tightly and was pleased when she let him.

Chapter Fourteen

Max didn't know how long he stood there and held Lola. He was peripherally aware of Stan and Sophie whispering nearby. Then Sophie made a call. After what could have been five minutes or fifteen, Max led Lola to the sofa and sat down there with her. He pulled her head into the crook of his neck and turned his face so he wouldn't have to look at Moore's body.

Stan and Sophie let them embrace in peace, and Max was grateful. He would have preferred they left him and Lola completely alone, but that wasn't possible, considering the dead gangster in their living room.

More time passed and more local police officers

arrived. That's when Max and Lola had to let go of each other and made their way outside. The coroner arrived. A short time later they met someone Sophie knew: a Captain Zacharias Bethel. A police photographer took pictures of the scene as the police huddled together.

Someone from the medical examiner's office arrived and loaded Moore onto a stretcher and wheeled him outside where a van was waiting. When the officers processing the scene seemed to be done, Sophie and Stan arrived with Captain Bethel, who looked at Max and Lola and simply said, "Tell me what happened here. And why was Henry Moore in your house? I assume this has something to do with the diamond."

"He asked me to help him steal it a week ago. I turned him down," Max said. He saw that Sophie was taking notes and continued. "He must've stolen it himself. Then he came back here to make sure there were no loose ends."

"Why didn't you come to me, tell me what they were planning?" Bethel said.

It was a fair question and Max was able to answer it honestly. "He said he'd kill us."

Stepping in, Sophie said, "You wouldn't have believed him anyway. You thought Moore was a second coming for this island," she said.

Well, he certainly would have been good for business at the police department. Crime would have been booming, Max mused to himself.

"Don't tell me what I thought. Where is the diamond?" he asked Max pointedly.

"Yeah, where is it?" Stan said.

"I have no idea," Max said innocently.

Two of the medical examiners lifted Moore's body and the stretcher into the van. Bethel turned to oversee them.

"They were trying to frame me," Max said to Stan.

"You know I don't buy a word of what you're saying," Stan said.

Fair enough. Max had given Stan plenty of reason to doubt his honesty. But what he had told them was partly true—hell, it was *mostly* true.

The two FBI agents, Kowalski and Stafford, arrived on the scene. "I want to take them in for more questioning," Kowalski said to Sophie.

"We'll question them more tomorrow. They've been through enough tonight," Sophie said.

Stafford stepped forward and said, "I don't think you understand, lady. I'm not asking you. I'm telling you."

Max could see that he had chosen precisely the wrong approach with Sophie, who was laying down a public challenge to Henry Moore the first time he saw her.

"I don't think *you* understand. You're in my jurisdiction," she said. Then she pointed to his gun and asked, "Did you register that weapon with local authorities when you arrived?"

Agent Stafford was suddenly unsure. "Ah, no," he said nervously.

"Then get off my island. Unless you want to spend a few nights with our local prison population. I'm sure they'd love to meet two clean-cut boys like you."

Something unspoken passed between the agents. Without another word, they turned and executed a strategic withdrawal. *Wise,* Max thought.

Bethel returned and said, "I want to bring them in. We still have a missing diamond, a dead man, and *you've* been involved the whole way."

"And as a result we've gotten rid of the biggest gangster on the island. A man you thought was a model citizen. Why don't you just go back to your desk and let the real cops do their jobs," Sophie said.

Max realized two things right away. First, there was some history between Bethel and Moore. And second, what Sophie said struck a nerve in Captain Bethel. All attention in the area was now drawn to Sophie and Bethel. Max saw that every cop in earshot was nodding his or her head in support of Sophie.

Bethel was completely at a loss for words.

Sophie turned to Stan and said, "Shall we?"

Stan took her arm and said, "We shall."

Then, arm in arm, they headed for her car and drove off together. Well, Stan might not have gotten his arrest, but he wasn't walking away with nothing. He and Sophie had found something in each other. To his surprise, Max found that he was happy for them.

Completely deflated, Bethel got into his own car and drove away. Max noticed that Lola had slipped away during the discussion. He went back into the house to look for her and saw that she was waiting at the door with her suitcase.

"You can't leave," he said.

"How can I stay?" she asked. Then she kissed him,

on the cheek. A soft, sad, good-bye kiss. "Good luck, Max," she said. Then she got into her car, started the engine, and drove off, her lights finally disappearing down the road.

Max stood there for a long time, too stunned to move. Even when she had thrown him out and he'd spent the night in Stan's suite, he had not really believed the break was permanent. He'd thought that when it was all over—when he had won the game he was playing—he would explain it all to her and she would be satisfied. Well, he'd told her the complete truth, he'd won the diamond, and he'd even—with help—beaten Moore. And yet he'd lost the one thing he knew he could not afford to lose.

He stepped back into the house. It was a mess. Furniture was overturned and there was blood on the floor where Moore had fallen. Ignoring it all, Max sat down on the couch. Hours later, he found himself wondering if he was wearing the same expression his father wore sitting in his easy chair, drinking himself into a quiet stupor each night. The thought gave him a chill as he looked out into the night sky though the window.

Was this his and Lola's last day together? He remembered their first day together, the day they'd met five years ago. The meeting was an accident, though in retrospect he realized that it was inevitable. Since then, he'd always believed it was fate.

A thief walks into a bar . . . Max had thought, smiling to himself as he stepped into the watering hole south of Dallas, Texas, called Stetson's. He'd chosen it carefully. It was quiet, out-of-the-way, and in a sleepy little town. And this time of day it wasn't very crowded, which meant he could control the events better and keep things from getting out of hand.

As he stepped inside, he heard the sound of country and western music and smelled the slightly stale smell of old beer. There was genuine sawdust on the floor and Max felt like he was walking onto a movie set instead of a real place. Behind the bar was the owner, a wiry man in his indeterminate forties who was completely bald. Sitting at the bar were two regulars. One was a bleached blonde, who was smoking, in her mid-thirties and just a few years past being genuinely pretty. The other was a tan heavyset man who arrived every day at four and usually stayed until closing.

The two regulars sat at the corners of the bar, and in the middle was a another customer, a thin man in his early thirties, reasonably fit and wearing jeans and a work shirt. His most distinguishing facial feature was a walrus-style mustache. Like the others, he kept to himself.

Nodding to the bartender, Max took a seat just one away from the mustached man, between him and the bleached blonde.

"What can I get you?" the bartender asked.

"Sweet vermouth, please," Max replied, putting on his best posh London accent.

"Excuse me?" the bartender asked, though with his accent it came out *scuuuz me.*

"Sweet vermouth, on the rocks, with a twist of lime," Max said politely.

"We've got the rocks and the lime, but no vermouth," the bartender said.

"Okay, how about a brandy," Max said.

"No brandy," the bartender said, annoyance creeping into his voice.

Good, Max thought. "I'll have a beer," Max said. "Do you have any imported . . ." Then he stopped, the look on the bartender's face telling him everything he needed to know. "Whatever you have on tap will be fine."

The bartender served up the beer, and before Max could take a sip, the mustached man next to him said, "You're not from around here, are you?"

"No," Max said.

"You're from England, ain't ya?" the man said.

"Yes, yes I am. North London, in fact," Max replied. "Have you ever been?"

"We don't get very many from North London in Conroe," the man said.

"I'm not surprised," Max said.

"Now why is that?" An edge crept into the voice.

That was good. Just what Max needed. It was time to stop playing around and pick a fight. "Not much out here, is there?" Max said.

"Now what do you mean?" the man said, a definite edge in his voice now.

"I mean there's not much of any interest," Max said, letting a bit of condescension creep into his own voice.

"See, that's where you're wrong. You've got farms and ranches, you've got your agriculture and animal husbandry and what not. You know anything about those things?" the man said.

Max raised his hands and said, "No offense. I'm sure this is a veritable cultural mecca of the agricultural arts, of which I am also sure you are a master."

The man stood, sliding the bar stool back away from him. It wouldn't be long now, Max realized. The edge in the man's voice was decidedly dangerous when he said, "Now, I've never been to North London. In fact, I've never been out of Texas, but I do know when I'm being insulted."

The bar had gone completely quiet, even the jukebox. Max could feel the eyes of the other three people in the bar on them. He didn't waste any time. He got up himself, now face-to-face with the mustached man, and said, "Well, then, you are not as ignorant as you look, but, of course, that would be impossible."

For a moment, the man looked at him uncomprehendingly. Max didn't wait. He wound up and socked the guy right on the chin. The man fell backward onto one of the tables behind him and then rolled to the floor. He got up surprisingly quickly and said, "You limey son of a bitch." Then he came out swinging, catching Max, hard, once on the cheek and once in the eye.

The next thing Max knew, he was on his knees, and the bartender and heavyset man were pulling the man off of him. "He's not worth it, Bud," he heard the bartender say.

Bud looked furious, but he allowed himself to be led back toward the exit by the heavyset man. "Why don't you go back where you came from, if you don't like it here?" Bud shouted at him from the other side of the bar.

Max got to his feet and said, "Excellent idea."

The bartender had come around to the front of the bar and put a hand on his shoulder and said, "You're not going anywhere, son. The sheriff will be here in a minute."

As it turned out, the sheriff arrived in half that time. As Max well knew, there was very little going on in Conroe, Texas, on a Wednesday evening at five o'clock.

"Now, what's all this fuss?" the sheriff asked.

Bud told his story. Then the others corroborated, saying that Max had picked a fight and then had hit Bud first. "This true?" the sheriff asked him.

"I was just minding my own business," Max said, then clammed up.

The sheriff wasn't buying it. He hauled Max in, photographed him, and booked him. "You want to confess?" the sheriff asked, good-naturedly.

"No, thank you," Max said as he stepped into his cell. The clock on the wall told him it was fifteen minutes to six. Fifteen minutes to closing time. Perfect. Max was right on schedule.

"You want to make a phone call?" The sheriff asked, handing Max a phone through the bars. He made a call to the office of a local lawyer, one that was on vacation.

"No one there," Max said. "I'll try him again in the morning."

"Okay, Mr. Burdett, it's dinnertime. Here's a menu from the local diner. Choose quick, the kitchen closes early." Max asked for a hamburger with fries and thanked the sheriff, who said, "Now, we'll take you to see the judge in the morning. Is there anything else you need?" Max shook his head no. "Alright. Now, I'm going to have a deputy bring your dinner in a bit. He'll also be in the office tonight. Yell out if you need anything, but you might have to shout. He's not supposed to sleep while he's supervising a prisoner, but he probably will."

"I'll be fine," Max said.

The sheriff looked him over. The man was polite and obviously in a rush to get home, but he was miles from stupid. Max was glad that the sheriff wouldn't be here tonight. "You're not going to make any trouble in my station house, are you?"

"No, sir. I'm looking forward to getting out of here and putting this all behind me," Max said.

"Okay, I'll see you tomorrow," the sheriff said.

Twenty minutes later, Deputy Steele brought him his dinner. It wasn't bad and Max ate the whole thing. A half hour later the deputy came back for the trash. And from what Max knew, that was the last time he would see anyone until morning. Of course, there was always a chance that something would go wrong and someone would stop by, but there was risk associated with every part of his job.

Max heard noises coming from the office until nine. Someone came to visit, and though Max couldn't hear, he knew it was the deputy's girlfriend. He also knew that she would stay for about two hours. Right on schedule, she left at eleven-thirty. Max waited another hour before making his move.

Standing on the bed, he opened the window. Beyond it, there were steel bars, more than thick enough to stop the drunks and brawlers who found themselves in this cell. Max reached outside and found the screwdriver he'd left under the windowsill. Working quickly, he removed with window's aluminum frame and pulled it inside the cell. Then he tested the bars. They felt solid when he tugged on them. Then he took his fist and rapped each corner one time. When he finished, the bars slid easily from the wall into his hands. They were heavy, so he maneuvered them carefully to the bed. That done, he pulled himself up to the open window frame and jumped into the alley outside.

Less than ten minutes after starting work, he was outside following his first jailbreak. It hadn't even been difficult; the trick was planning it in advance and making a few preparations. And Max excelled at both.

He felt a sense of urgency now and moved quickly. He still had a lot of ground to cover before morning. He walked to his car and got the things he needed from the trunk. Then he returned to his cell where he put the full-size dummy in the bed, covering it up. Then he put the tape recorder under the blanket and turned it on. Immediately the low sound of his own snoring filled the room. Now in the unlikely event that the deputy checked the cell, he would see and hear a sleeping man in the bed. The deputy would have to enter the cell and shake him to see through the ruse, and Max was confident that wouldn't happen.

Then he reset the window and bars temporarily from the outside, and Max was in his car and on his way before one a.m. He drove on to the North Dallas area, and sixty-five minutes later parked in the municipal lot next to the train station in Plano. There were a few cars there, so his wouldn't stick out. But even if it did, the car was clean and untraceable to him. Later, he would be using a different car to drive back to Conroe, one that had been sitting in the same lot for days.

He put on his black clothes and got out of the car, carrying everything he needed in his backpack. The walk to the bank was less than ten minutes. He slipped around back where he used the fire escape to get to the roof. From there, it was a simple matter to disconnect the alarm and security cameras and then jimmy the skylight. After a few minutes, he stood, alone, in the lobby of the bank.

The security had been easy to breach, but Max didn't blame the bank. The vault door was first-rate and protected the bank's cash very well. But Max wasn't after the cash—too bulky in large amounts for him, anyway. He moved quickly and traveled light; thus, he rarely went after cash.

He made his way to the back of the bank and took the stairs down to the basement level, where the safety deposit boxes were kept. They were protected by a very thick steel door that had two solid deadbolts. The locks were tough and would have stopped all but the most determined and skilled thieves. It took Max a full ten minutes to get through them.

Opening the door, he stepped through and got his first surprise on this job so far. There was an insistent beeping sound. He found the source on a wall nearby.

There was a flashing red light above the keypad that he did not expect to be there. Before it had fully registered what was going on, Max tore into his backpack and pulled out his PDA, which he'd customized. It had a faster processor than most high-end desktop computers and specialized decryption software on which his entire future was about to depend.

He estimated about ten seconds had passed, which meant he had only fifty seconds to enter the correct code. He tore the plastic face off of the keypad, then used the clips wired to the PDA to insert into the right spots on the keypad's circuit board. He knew the model alarm, so he found what he was looking for almost immediately and switched on the software, estimating that he had maybe thirty or thirty-five seconds before the alarm sounded.

He considered aborting the job right now. For this time of night, at this distance from the police station, response time would be perhaps four minutes. He wouldn't bother trying to get back out the skylight and would head out the front door—no longer having to worry about the main alarm. Still, he would have to get far away from the bank, but it was the middle of the night and no one else was out. Anyone caught on the street would be a suspect. The extra thirty seconds might easily be what he needed to escape. Given the level of encryption on this alarm system, his PDA would need a full ninety seconds to try every numerical combination.

Of course, it might hit on the correct code in the thirty-five seconds he had . . .

Or not.

Max realized that his decision had already been made and he stood his ground. He planned each job meticulously, but there were almost always surprises. He dealt with them as best he could and trusted his instincts when trouble arose. Now his instincts were telling him that he would be okay.

He watched the clock on the PDA's screen and counted off the seconds. Twenty left.

Then fifteen . . .

Then ten . . .

Five . . .

For a moment, Max wondered if he'd been wrong here. His instincts had never led him wrong before, but he wondered for moment if the jails were full of men who could say the same thing.

Four . . .

Three. And then a beep from the PDA. Immediately, Max hit the return button and the computer fed the code into the alarm system.

Max took a sigh of relief as the red light above the keypad turned green. He was in. Closing the door quietly, Max took a step into the safety deposit box room. There were dozens of boxes, but Max was only interested in one of them. He scanned quickly for the correct row and number, which he had memorized.

And then Max got the second surprise of the job. There was a strong thud coming from beneath him. It was muffled, but Max had a sinking feeling that he knew exactly what it was. He wouldn't take off until he knew what he was dealing with, but Max was pretty sure he was about to have company.

Sure enough, a few seconds later the storeroom door at the other end of the room opened. A small cloud of dust entered the room, and behind it he saw a figure dressed in black, wearing a black mask—looking a lot like him, he realized. The third surprise of the day was that the figure was female, very female, and was looking at him unflinchingly.

Max decided to bluff. "I've called the police, are on their way," he said, trying to sound official, as if he belonged here—though he knew that the black mask and clothes he was wearing were playing hell with his credibility.

The woman in front of him laughed, a surprisingly gentle sound given the circumstances. "Then you had better get out of here before you get caught," she said, a hint of an accent in her voice. *Spanish,* he thought. The voice was pleasant, but firm. She wasn't going to cut and run herself. But she also wasn't moving against him.

If she had a gun, this job would be over for him, since he didn't carry them himself. When she didn't produce one, Max felt himself relaxing. Perhaps he could still salvage the job.

"Look, I think we're both here for the same reason and I don't mind telling you that I'm in a bit of a hurry. I only want one of the boxes, the rest are yours," Max said. He was on a very tight schedule. He couldn't afford a half hour of wrangling with a competitor.

"That's fine, as long as the one you want isn't the one containing the Felbrant jewels," she said amiably. "That one's mine."

Max felt his heart sink a bit. Whoever this was, she

wasn't stupid. She'd obviously followed the Felbrant case and was professional enough to blast into here from the subbasement. "Coincidentally, the Felbrant jewels are why I'm here as well," Max said, keeping his own voice friendly.

The Felbrant case had been making the local Dallas headlines for months. A Dallas oilman had married a much younger woman and then died six months later. His children were contesting the will and trying to get ahold of all his important assets, including jewelry owned by the oilman's first wife—jewelry that was no doubt worth more than the contents of all the other safety deposit boxes combined.

"Looks like we have a problem," she said. Her voice was low and sexy and the accent made her sound damned exotic. Max found himself wondering what she looked like under that mask. Smiling, he took a step forward and saw that her eyes were dark.

Max shook his head. It wasn't like him to get distracted on a job—even by an attractive woman. But he realized that she was more than just an attractive woman. She was an attractive woman who was a competitor— playing perhaps at his own level. That was an intriguing combination.

"A problem . . . or an opportunity. Look, neither one of us has a gun or we would have pulled it already. So it looks like we will both have to call it a day, or split the jewels," he said.

"Are you kidding?" she said.

"You have another solution?" he shot back. Then he checked his watch. "Neither one of us has much time."

She thought about that for a moment and then said. "Fifty-fifty?" she said.

"Of course," he replied.

"I've never had a full partner before," she said.

"It will be a new experience for both of us," Max replied.

"If you try anything, you'll regret it," she said. It was a statement, not a threat or a boast, but Max didn't doubt her for a second. She was petite, maybe five-two, but she had already given him a rather big surprise today. He was in no rush to set himself up for another one.

"Don't trust me?" he asked lightly.

"Well, all I know about you is that you're a thief—a pretty good one or you wouldn't be here. On the other hand, it looks like you almost missed the new alarm." She looked over his shoulder at the keypad and added, "And I'm betting you had to white-knuckle the decryption on that one."

"Well, no job ever goes perfectly," he said, pointing to himself and then to her. "I think we've both gotten surprises today."

She checked her own watch and said, "Okay, let's do this quickly." She found the right spot on the wall and pulled out her own locksmith tools—nickel-plated, probably alloy underneath, clearly a custom set like his own. "I'll get the box."

Max nodded and watched her work. She had good hands and had the small door open and the box on the floor in under a minute. Max crouched down next to her as she opened it. The jewels were all there, as near as he could tell. It was the most amazing collection of estate jewelry that he had ever seen. Many of the pieces were famous in their own right, with interesting histories. All of them were exceptional.

"We could haggle all night, but I suggest that we just take turns, one piece at a time," she said.

Max nodded. "Ladies first," he said.

His competitor immediately went to the most valuable piece in the box, a ruby broach. It was not the biggest or flashiest, but it had some of the best gem-quality rubies he had ever seen. Max was impressed; this woman knew what she was doing. If he was going to have to share the spoils of a job, better to share with someone he could at least respect. Max took the next most valuable piece in the collection; then she chose again. And so on until they had cleaned out the box.

When they were done, they both got up, and Max said, "One question. Plastic explosives, in the subbasement? Tricky and loud."

She nodded, "Yeah, but I didn't have to play with the alarm. And if you know your way around shape-charges, you can get away with it."

Max thought back to all the big jobs in the last year or two that used explosives and wondered if she had run them. From what he'd seen, none of them were beyond her abilities. "I'd like to say that it's been nice to meet you, but . . ."

"Yeah, same here," she said, turning for the storage room door. Then she turned back and said, "Why don't you borrow my escape route? It'll save you having to climb back up to the roof. That is how you got in, isn't it?"

"Yes, and thank you," Max said, following her through

the hole in the floor, down a service corridor, and out a basement window. On the street, they walked through the alley and hit the street. Out in the open, Max took off his mask and waited for her to do the same.

She hesitated, as if she didn't want her to see him. "You've seen me," he said. Still, she thought it over, but common sense won out. On a job, a mask was useful in case there were witnesses or a hidden security camera. On the street, they might as well be neon signs announcing THIEF!

Slowly she took off her mask, and Max saw her face for the first time. She was beautiful. Dark Latin skin and the large eyes that he had already seen. For a moment, Max's breath caught in his throat.

"You're staring," she said.

"Sorry, but most of the people in my line of work are more . . . Well, they're less . . . female," he said, smiling.

Before she could respond, a car approached. Max didn't hesitate; he reached for her and pulled her toward him. She understood what he was doing and even helped, but then she looked up at him and said, "If you try anything you'll regret it."

Max believed her, but found that he was still tempted to kiss her. Up close, she smelled wonderful and there was a hint of a smile on her lips as she watched him. "Just business, until they pass," he said.

When the car was gone, he let her go, and they headed farther down the street. "I'm in the municipal lot, by the train station," he said.

"Me, too," she said.

They walked in silence and Max realized that in a

minute or two he would never see her again. "Could I call you?" Max asked. He knew it sounded lame, but he had never met someone like her before. Relationships were difficult in his line of work, and it was impossible to trust an ordinary woman with a number of very important truths about himself.

"Are you serious?" she asked.

"Yes," he said.

"Looking for a chance to take back my half for yourself?" she asked.

"No. I thought we could get together. Why don't you go stash your share? I'll do the same. I'm staying the night in Conroe." Then he took out a pen and pad and wrote down the address. "I'll be here until about ten-thirty," he said, handing her the paper. She looked at him like he was insane. "Look, you surprised me tonight, a few times, and a few of those surprises were even pleasant. I don't mind saying that I'm intrigued and more than a little interested. Like I said, I'll be there until ten-thirty. Stop by, we'll have . . . lunch. The local diner isn't bad."

Before she could say anything, he jumped in his car and pulled out as she watched him from the sidewalk. He made even better time on his drive back to Conroe, even with a stop to stash the jewels. Usually, he used the time after a job to review details and evaluate his own performance. This time, he found that he was thinking only of her.

Back at the jail, he slipped inside and made sure the small piece of tape he'd put on the cell door hadn't been broken. It was intact, which meant that no one had checked the cell. Then he put the dummy into the car and grabbed the small paper bag he needed.

Back inside his cell, he mixed the industrial epoxy he put in the bag and reset the bars on their frame. They wouldn't be quite as strong as before, but they would look convincing from either the inside or the outside. In the unlikely event that in the future a petty criminal in that cell yanked the bars hard enough to dislodge them, Max would be a long way away. Next he used the screwdriver to put the window frame back in place, and then put the screwdriver in the bag with the remains of the epoxy. Finally, he threw the bag into the trash can underneath the window. He left the window open to clear out the smell of the epoxy and sat down on the bed.

According to the clock on the wall, it was just after five, meaning he had about twenty-five minutes until sunrise, which had been his deadline for getting everything finished. Max relaxed. He had gotten himself thrown into jail, busted out, and then stolen the jewels. The hard part was over. The only thing left now was getting out of here.

As he lay down, he realized that he was looking forward to the morning. Usually, he spent the day after a job fencing his goods, but he hoped he would have something even more interesting to do today. As he closed his eyes, he found he had only one thought and wanted only one thing: to find out what was behind that smile he had seen last night.

The sheriff didn't wake him until almost nine-thirty, for which Max was grateful. "Morning, Mr. Burdett.

You've got yourself a lucky break. Bud from the bar last night stopped by and dropped all the charges," he said, opening the cell door.

"Really?" Max said, trying to sound surprised.

"Yup. Apparently, he had to leave town and doesn't want to be bothered with the hearing or the follow-up," the sheriff said.

"Am I free to go?" Max asked.

"Well, there's the small matter of damage in the bar. Two hundred and fifty dollars for a table and a chair," the sheriff said.

"How soon can I pay it?" Max asked.

"The town clerk is Dan from the bar's brother-in-law, so he'll take the money if you want," the sheriff said.

"Fine," Max said, checking his watch.

"After that, we'll have you processed and out of here in no time." The sheriff had been as good as his word. Max paid the clerk, filled out a few forms, and had gotten his personal effects back all by ten-twenty. He'd waited a few minutes for the sheriff, who finally said, "Come on, let's get you out of here." Outside, the sun was shining and it was already eighty-some degrees outside.

Scanning the area, he saw what he was looking for, leaning against the car and watching him. Max couldn't help but smile. The sheriff noticed and said, "If I had a woman like that waiting for me, I'd try to stay out of trouble."

"I think you're right about that, Sheriff," Max said.

"In the future, if you want to insult these parts in particular or Texas in general, I'd do it from a couple of states away," the sheriff said.

"You know, Sheriff, I have to admit that Texas has been nothing but good to me since I got here," Max said.

"Then you stay out of trouble," the sheriff said.

"I'll try, Sheriff, and thanks," Max replied, heading for the woman waiting for him.

"It's a little early for lunch," she said, smiling.

"How about a late breakfast?" he asked.

Nodding toward the police station, she asked, "What was all that about?"

"My alibi for the night," he replied.

For the first time since he'd met her, she looked impressed. "A pretty good one," she said.

"They're my specialty," Max said.

At the diner, they ordered food and she asked him, "So what do you have in mind?"

"Ever been to Morocco?"

"No, but I hear it's nice," she said.

And that was it. The Morocco job had been their first date. On the way to the diner, she had asked, "What exactly are you proposing?"

"A partnership," Max had said.

"Personal or professional?" she asked. Her tone was light but he knew it was a serious question.

"Is there a difference?" he asked.

Five years later he had finally learned the difference. Unfortunately, he had come by the wisdom a bit too late. *Too soon old, and too late smart,* the saying went. It fit him perfectly.

Too late . . .

Chapter Fifteen

Max got up from the chair and stepped outside onto the new deck where he saw something truly amazing. The red sun was rising out of the Caribbean Sea. As the sun rose higher in the sky, the sky and clouds turned red and orange, the colors slowly chasing each other in a widening arc. It was beautiful, amazing actually, and Max realized that this was the first sunrise he'd ever watched.

Still haven't watched the sun set, a voice inside him said. And in that moment, he realized the voice was not his own; it was Lola's. Suddenly, the deck at sunrise with beauty all around him seemed like the loneliest place in the world.

So do something about it, the voice said.

Then a plan began to form in his mind. Well, *plan* was a generous term for what he had in mind. There was no time for proper planning. And he would be operating well out of his comfort zone, where none of the skills he'd honed in his career would be of much use.

It would be improvisation all the way, with a real chance of failure. Nevertheless, Max decided that maybe he wasn't retired after all. Perhaps he still had one more job in him, this time for the whole pot.

Back in the house, Max looked at his phone and computer. Not surprisingly, Lola had gone off the grid. She wasn't registered anywhere and hadn't spent a dime on her credit card. *She doesn't want to be found,* he realized. That meant only one thing: she was on the run.

Max checked schedules for the airport and the seaport. Both had early flights, and there was only time for him to reach one of them—with no way to tell which one she would take. So Max did what he always did on a job when faced with a time-sensitive choice and inadequate information: he guessed, trusting his instincts and what he knew about Lola.

Max hopped in his car and raced for the seaport. Checking his watch, Max saw that he had no time to spare. At the seaport, he pulled up to the dock and jumped out of the car. He saw the plane in position to depart and ran for it. As he got closer, he saw Lola in the crowd waiting to board the plane. Max thought about calling out to her but was afraid she'd duck inside, so he poured on the speed.

He was almost there when she handed her suitcase to

an attendant, who put it in the cargo hold. Lola stepped toward the small ramp that led to the seaplane door. Just as she got near it, Max reached out his hand for her and said, "Lola, wait."

She turned and saw him behind her. He was disappointed that her face was still cold to him, but he had known that this wouldn't be easy. When she turned back to the plane, he took her arm. "Hear me out," he said.

"It's not going to work, Max. Not this time," she said.

"Please," he said.

Something in his tone made her hesitate and he didn't waste the opportunity. "I know it's too late, but I finally wrote them," he said, pulling out a crumpled piece of paper filled with his writing. "See? Lots of words. But I don't have to read them, because I know it by heart."

Lowering the paper, Max said, "A man only has two important things in his life: his work and his love. When he's done with one, if he's lost the other, then he's got nothing; he is nothing. And that's what happened to me . . ." Taking a step toward her, he continued, "I've spent my whole life chasing things I thought were valuable when the only thing I really care about was right in front of me all along."

Max took Lola's hand and said, "From this moment on, you're my only jewel. I want a life filled with sunsets. And I don't want to watch one of them without you. Not ever."

Reaching into his pocket, Max pulled out the ring he'd been carrying for weeks now. As she looked down on it, something moved on Lola's face. "The first diamond I've ever *bought*." Then, knowing that a better time would never come, Max said, "Lola Cirillo, marry me tomorrow."

She looked at the ring, then up at him, and he saw it. The flash in her eyes, the pleasure at seeing him. The dam had broken and Max didn't waste the moment. Leaning down, he kissed her deeply. In mid-kiss, she pushed him away, and for a terrible moment, Max thought something was wrong.

"On one condition," Lola said.

"Anything," Max said, meaning it.

Pointing to the diamond ring, Lola smiled slightly and said, "I want to see the receipt."

Then they both smiled, broadly, and kissed again. Max was only vaguely aware of the seaplane taking off and flying into the horizon behind them.

They slept into the afternoon and then stayed in bed for a couple more hours. Then Lola shooed him out of the house to make some preparations, and he decided to stop by the tiki bar at the Atlantis. He was pleased to see Luc behind the counter—that meant he could tie up one of his last loose ends tonight. Slapping his hand down on the bar, Max said, "Jack on the rocks. With an umbrella. What the hell—I'm celebrating." Luc nodded and Max continued, "And congratulations, Luc. As of five o'clock today, you own this place."

Luc smiled widely now. It was more than they had agreed to, by a significant margin, but Max couldn't have done the job without him. "Wow, man. Thanks," Luc said.

"I always take care of my friends," Max said, smiling.

Suddenly, a hand fell on Max's shoulder. "Forget the Jack on the rocks. Let's have Remoras all round!" the voice behind him said. It was Stan.

Max turned to see him. He hadn't had a chance to thank Stan for saving them from Moore—and to apologize for the way things had gone down. But Stan was smiling, and there, on his wrist, was a brand new Panerai watch. It was exactly like Max's own.

"Check this out, man. I treated myself. Maxed out the credit cards. Suits me, don't you think?" Stan asked.

It didn't make sense. That watch would have cost most of a year's take-home if he was working at the FBI—and Stan was on suspension. "That must take a bite out of a government salary," he said.

"Oh, I can afford it alright," Stan said. There was something different about Stan. Gone was his bitterness, the desperate edge that had been in his voice lately.

Luc put down the Remoras in front of them, and Stan said, "Have a sip of your Remora and we'll talk about it."

Max hesitated. Something strange was going on here. Stan leaned over and plucked out the umbrella for him. With a shrug, Max sipped the drink. It was fruity but surprisingly mild. Looking at Stan, he said, "Thought you said these had kick?" Stan was smiling, and suddenly Max was sure that something was very wrong here. Then he turned to Luc and said, "Luc, what's in this thing?"

"Orange juice, mango juice, grenadine, coconut milk," Luc said.

Suddenly Max understood, not everything—not all the details—but the most important thing of all: Stan had played him somehow. He'd done it well and was now looking like the cat who'd swallowed the canary.

"No liquor?" Max asked.

Luc shook his head. "Nada," Stan offered.

Suddenly, Max had flashes of the events that night when he'd thought Stan was drunk. He remembered Stan, looking completely wasted, shouting out, *"Gimme a Remora!"* He'd remembered carrying Stan back to his hotel room. He even remembered smelling liquor on him. Then after he wrestled Stan into his bed, he had covered the man up and turned to Luc and had said, *"Tell anyone I tucked him in, I'll kill you."*

Max and Luc had left after that, but Max now knew what must have happened next. He imagined a very sober Stan opening his eyes and following him.

"You okay? You don't look too good," Stan asked.

Suddenly, Max didn't feel so good. After he'd left the hotel, Max had gone to the cove to check on the Zodiac. Stan must have seen the bones of Max's plan. Even if Stan hadn't figured out all the details immediately, he would have seen enough to prepare . . . something. Whatever it was, Max could tell by Stan's face that the agent was pretty damned pleased with himself.

"You know, I really liked that cove . . ." Stan said, as if reading Max's mind.

Max remembered using a drill later that night to hollow out a hiding place for the diamond under the pier. He imagined Stan watching every movement, knowing where the diamond would be even if he didn't know Max's whole plan. A heavy ball settled in Max's stomach and he felt himself start to sweat.

"I liked it so much I went back there this morning," Stan said, his voice a taunt.

Max imagined Stan there in the morning light, pulling out the diamond and opening the pouch to hold in his hands something worth much more than he would make in a hundred years on his government salary.

Stan gestured to the drink. "As an underwater enthusiast, you should know what a remora really is, Max. You know your shark, the one who does what he's born to do? Well the remora is a kind of a stowaway. A suckerfish that sticks to the shark's body and feeds off it. The shark does all the work, but the remora gets the spoils . . ."

As Stan smiled his victor's smile, the rest of the missing pieces fell into place in Max's mind. He remembered looking at the Napoleon III diamond for the first time in the ship's exhibit room.

"You're gonna be bored. I'm just here to look," Max had said.

Then he remembered when he stole the schematics and planted the fibers he'd taken from Moore's clothing. That night, Sophie had gotten the drop on him. She had him dead to rights, gun drawn and pointed at him.

And then Stan had intervened. At the time, Max had thought that Stan had just bumbled into the way, ruining Sophie's bust. It should have been the last mistake of Max's career, *but Stan had let him go.* The idea took some getting used to. Stan might have been watching him before, but that could simply have just been police work. But from the point that Stan stopped Sophie from making her arrest, Max had been playing Stan's game.

That hit him right in his pride, but to Max's surprise the hit wasn't that bad. He'd known from the beginning that taking the diamond was not a one-man job—of course, unwitting fools like Jean-Paul didn't count as partners. Stan might have let Max go, but he'd never have even gotten close if Max and Lola had worked the job together.

"You did it, Stan. You set me up. Right from the start," Max said.

Stan was grinning widely. "I revel in it. I revel in it," Stan said.

Reflexively, Max chastised himself for not recovering the diamond immediately, but then he realized that Stan would have known he had it and would have had cause to make an arrest. And more importantly, Max never would have come to his understanding with Lola. On balance, Max thought he'd come out ahead.

And he'd taken enough from Stan over the years. The agent might as well have this one victory. Max merely smiled.

"You see that? You lost," Stan said.

"No I didn't. I got Lola," Max said simply.

Stan looked mildly disappointed, as disappointed as a man could be when he had just gotten his hands on a fortune. Max was glad to let Stan go, but he found that he wanted to see Lola.

Stan raised his voice to stop him. "One other thing. You said a fence would only give ya twenty for it. Well I got a fence lined up in Chicago who's gonna give me thirty."

"Really? You'll have to introduce me to him sometime," Max said lightly and got up. As he turned to go, he saw Stan take a slug of his Remora.

"Ah, that's good," Stan said behind him.

"See you at the house later," Max called back.

"I'll be there," Stan said, his voice somewhere between thrilled and ecstatic.

At home, Sophie met Max at the door and kept him outside. "She's getting ready," Sophie said.

"What about me?" Max said.

Sophie disappeared behind the door and came back a minute later holding out some clothes for him on hangers. Max got dressed around back and waited, watching the ocean. Later on, Stan had showed up with Luc, and the three men waited together.

Finally, Sophie came around to get them, and they all headed out to the deck, where Lola was waiting. For a second, when Max saw her, his breath caught in his throat. She looked amazing, in a beautiful dress that he didn't know she had. The sun was behind her, dancing off her dark hair.

Max was never in his life as sure as he was then that he was doing the right thing. A local minister arrived. Sophie put on some music and then Stan took him to stand in front of the minister. Running back to Lola, Stan held out his arm. Lola took it and they walked together up the aisle.

Max kept his eyes on Lola. She was beaming, and he knew he was wearing a big, silly grin on his own face. With his peripheral vision, he saw that the workmen who had delivered the lumber for the deck had come by to look on.

The ceremony was short. They read their vows and Stan produced the wedding rings. In less than a half hour they were married. Max leaned down to kiss her and thought that it was the best use of a half hour he could think of. Then, when the kiss broke, Lola looked at him with a gleam in her eye, and Max thought of something even better they could do.

It would have to wait, of course. A truck from a local restaurant arrived and then the place was swarming with servers. The guests stayed for about two hours and then Max and Lola were alone.

"Well," Lola said, "aren't you going to carry me over the threshold?

"Not yet," Max replied. She looked at him in disbelief, but he held out his hand and led her around back to the hammock. "It's almost time for the sunset. I thought we could catch this one."

Lola hadn't said a word. She merely lay down beside him and they spent the next half hour watching the light show in the sky.

"What did you think?" Lola asked when it was done.

"Nice, if you like that sort of thing," Max said, smiling.

"Well, what sort of thing do you like, Mr. Burdett?" she asked playfully.

"Actually, Mrs. Burdett, it's easier if I show you," Max said, getting up and lifting her off the hammock.

Epilogue

Stan, feeling like the cat that caught the canary, reclined in the backseat of the huge stretch limo. The limo's bar had been ransacked, and Stan was just popping open another bottle of champagne as the limo pulled onto the tarmac, heading toward the private Lear jet that sat at the runway's edge.

Holding his cell phone to his ear, Stan took a sip of bubbly and said, "I'm holding the diamond in my hand. My plane takes off in ten minutes. Tomorrow morning, the bidding will start at thirty million dollars." He took another hearty swig, gulping down the sweet taste of success. "And if I were you," he added, "I'd bring cash."

Stan closed his phone and held the diamond up to the light streaming through the limo's window. The facets caused lights to dance in front of his eyes, points of rainbow lights dancing around the limo's interior. Stan was nearly giddy. His payday had finally arrived.

Back at their beach house, Max and Lola were also reclined, on their deck in front of the brilliant umber and rose hues of a glorious island sunset.

"Well," Max said, "you win some, you lose some."

"We still have sunsets, Max," Lola said.

"Yeah. Forever."

They smiled at each other, basking in the warm glow of a burning sun slowly sliding into the horizon.

"And hey, don't worry," Lola said. "One day you'll find a hobby."

Max picked up his PDA, which had been sitting on his lap. "You know, I think I already have."

At that, Max hit a button on his handheld.

The limo driver was just finishing getting Stan's bag from the trunk as Stan was just finishing the champagne. With the final remnants, Stan held his glass aloft in a toast. "Goodbye, paradise!" he exclaimed, and drained his glass.

Turning to get out, Stan tried the door—but found it locked. Reaching across to the other passenger door, he found himself unable to open it, either. "What the . . ." Stan exclaimed.

Abruptly, the limo shifted into gear, its driver's seat empty, and the gas pedal automatically hit the floor. With screeching tires and smoking rubber, the limo lurched forward, throwing Stan back against the seat and sending him sprawling. The limo had turned away from the jet and was headed back the way they had come on the access road.

"Max! Max, you son of a bitch!" Stan yelled at the top of his lungs as the limo careened away.

Max winked at Lola, punching away at buttons on his PDA.

"The last time, right Max?" Lola said.

"Last time."